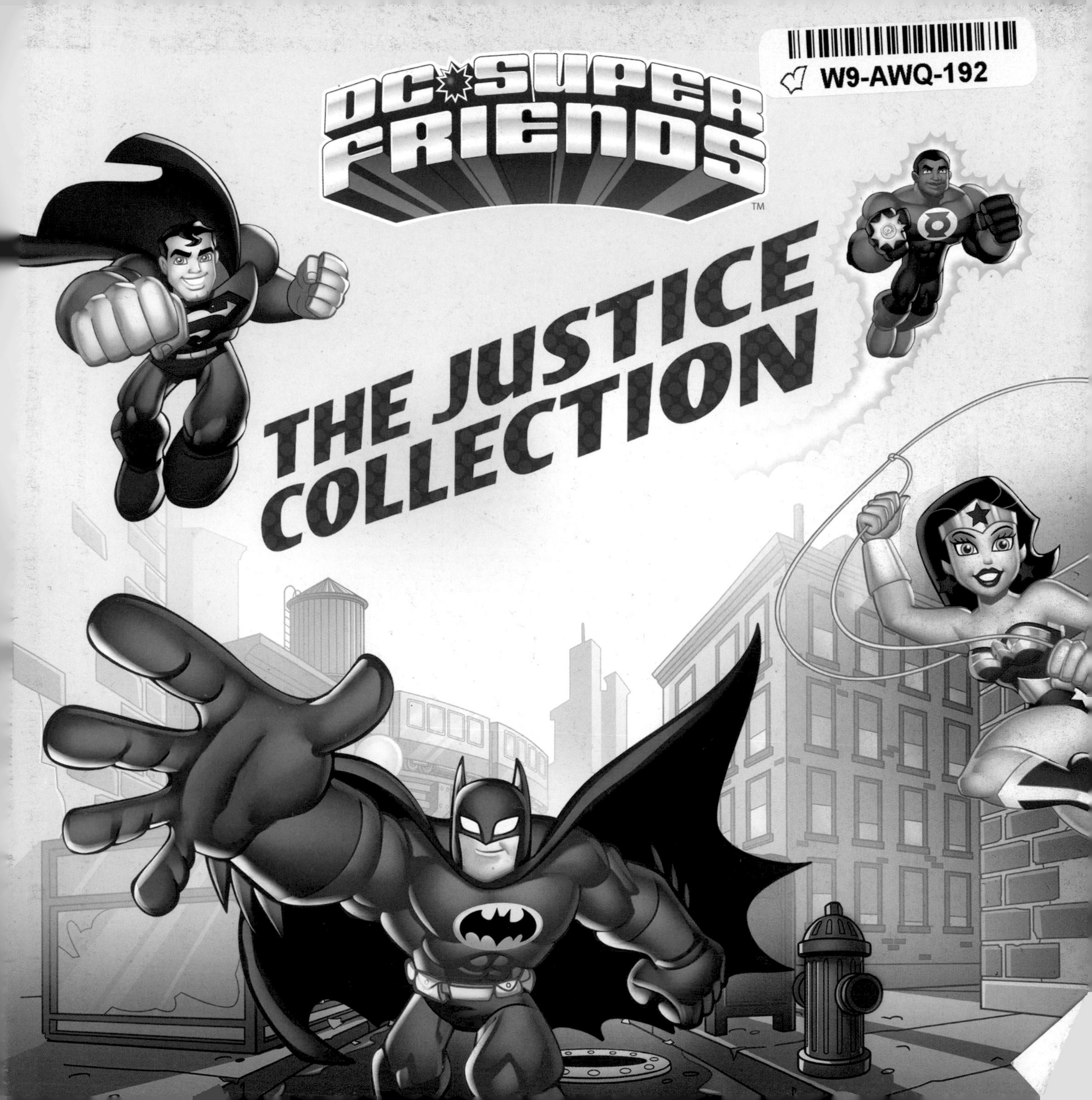
DC SUPER FRIENDS™
THE JUSTICE COLLECTION

A Random House PICTUREBACK® Book

Random House 🏠 New York

All rights reserved. Published in the United States by Random House Children's Books, a division of Penguin Random House LLC,
1745 Broadway, New York, NY 10019, and in Canada by Penguin Random House Canada Limited, Toronto. These stories were
originally published separately in different form by Random House as *Heroes United!/Attack of the Robot!* in 2008, *Green Lantern
vs. the Meteor Monster!* in 2011, *Jailbreak!* in 2014, and *Battle in Space!* in 2015. Pictureback, Random House, and the
Random House colophon are registered trademarks of Penguin Random House LLC.

randomhousekids.com

ISBN 978-1-5247-6878-2

MANUFACTURED IN CHINA

10 9 8 7 6 5 4 3 2 1

CONTENTS

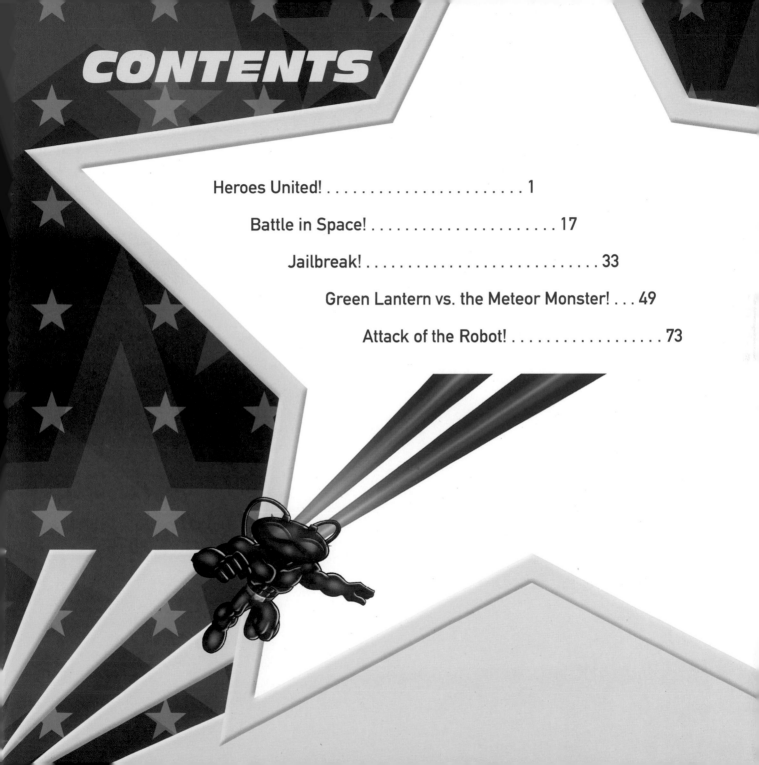

Heroes United! 1

Battle in Space! 17

Jailbreak! 33

Green Lantern vs. the Meteor Monster! . . . 49

Attack of the Robot! 73

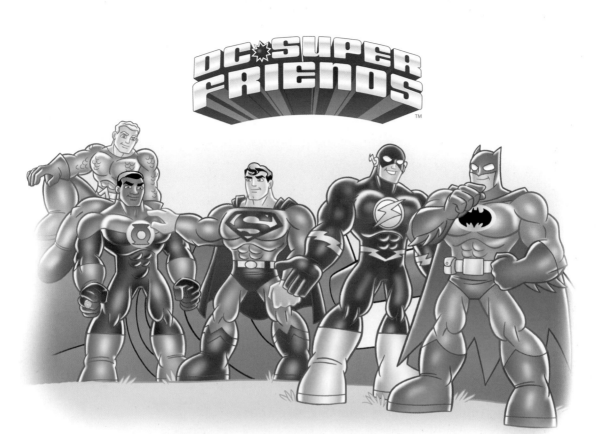

Heroes United!

By Dennis "Rocket" Shealy

Illustrated by Erik Doescher, Mike DeCarlo, and David Tanguay

In times of trouble, the world's mightiest super heroes, each with his own unique powers and abilities, unite to help save the day.

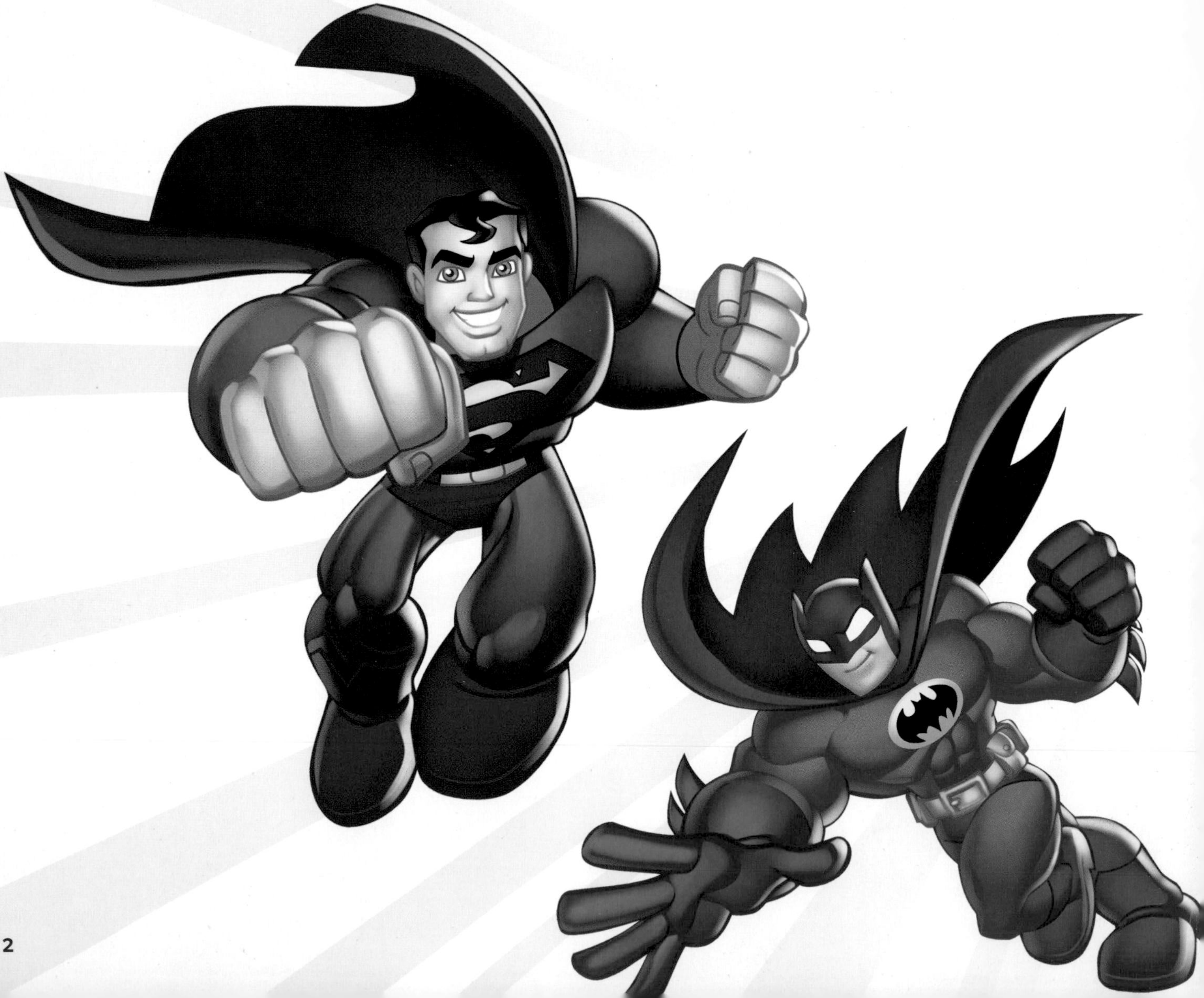

Together these heroes are a winning team that stands for truth and justice. They are . . . **the Super Friends!**

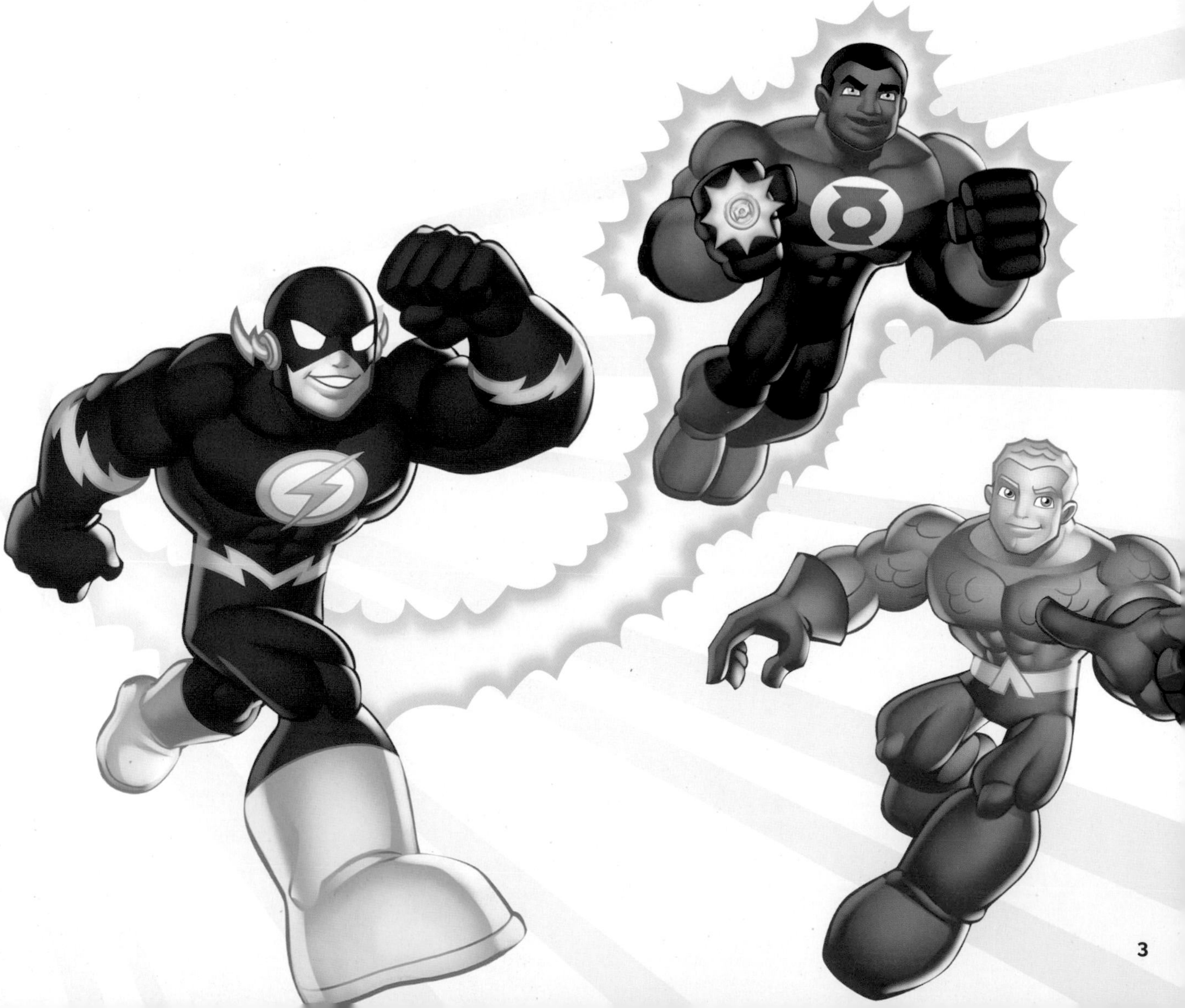

SUPERMAN

Superman is the Man of Steel. He is incredibly strong. He can lift heavy objects, such as buses and big train engines. He flies faster than the fastest jet, and he can see through walls with his X-ray vision. He can even use his chilly superbreath to put bad guys on ice!

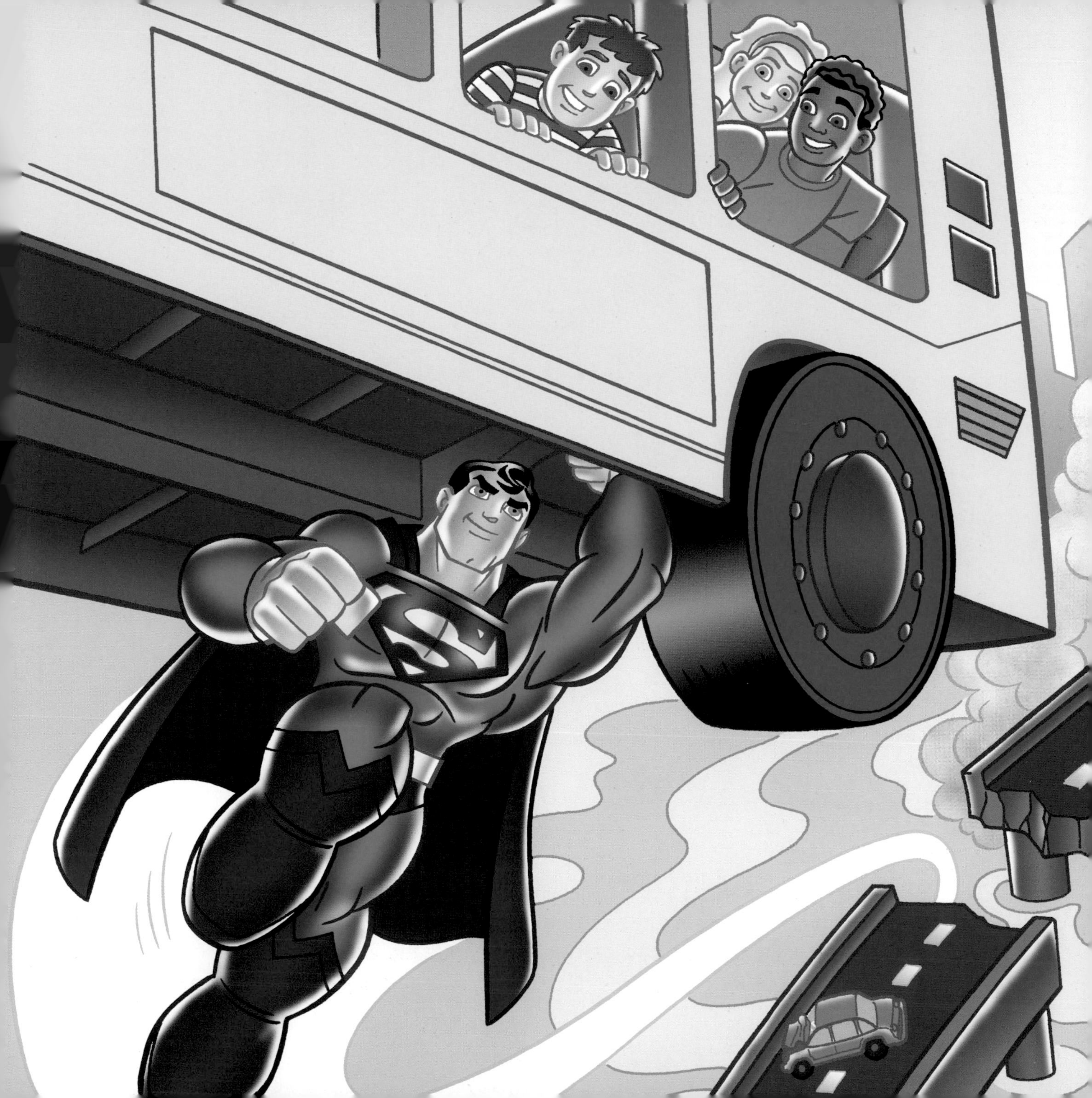

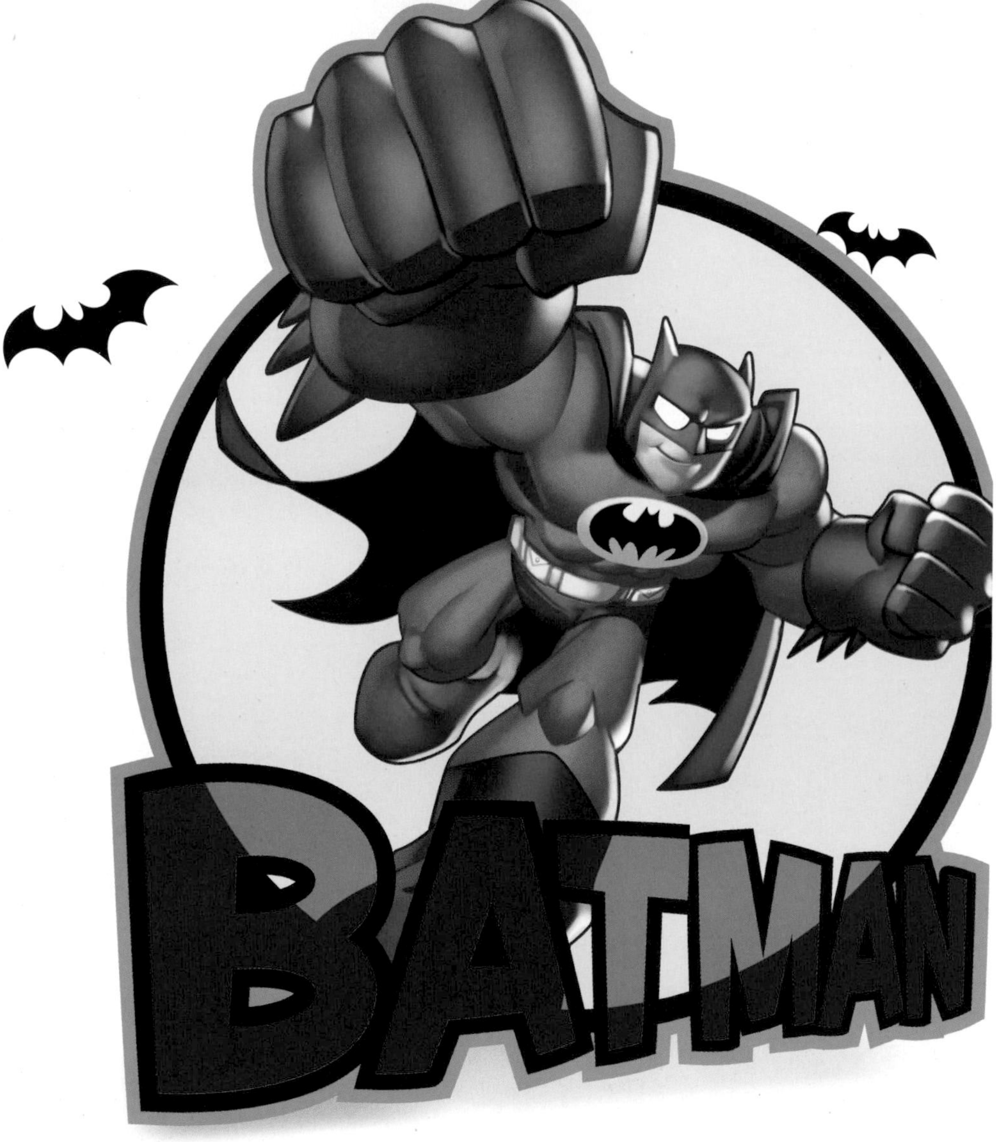
BATMAN

Batman is also known as the Caped Crusader and the Dark Knight. He keeps Gotham City safe using his Utility Belt, which is full of Batarangs, Batropes, and other high-tech gadgets. Batman patrols the city streets at night on his Batcycle or in the rocket-powered Batmobile. Bad guys, beware—no one can escape when Batman is in pursuit!

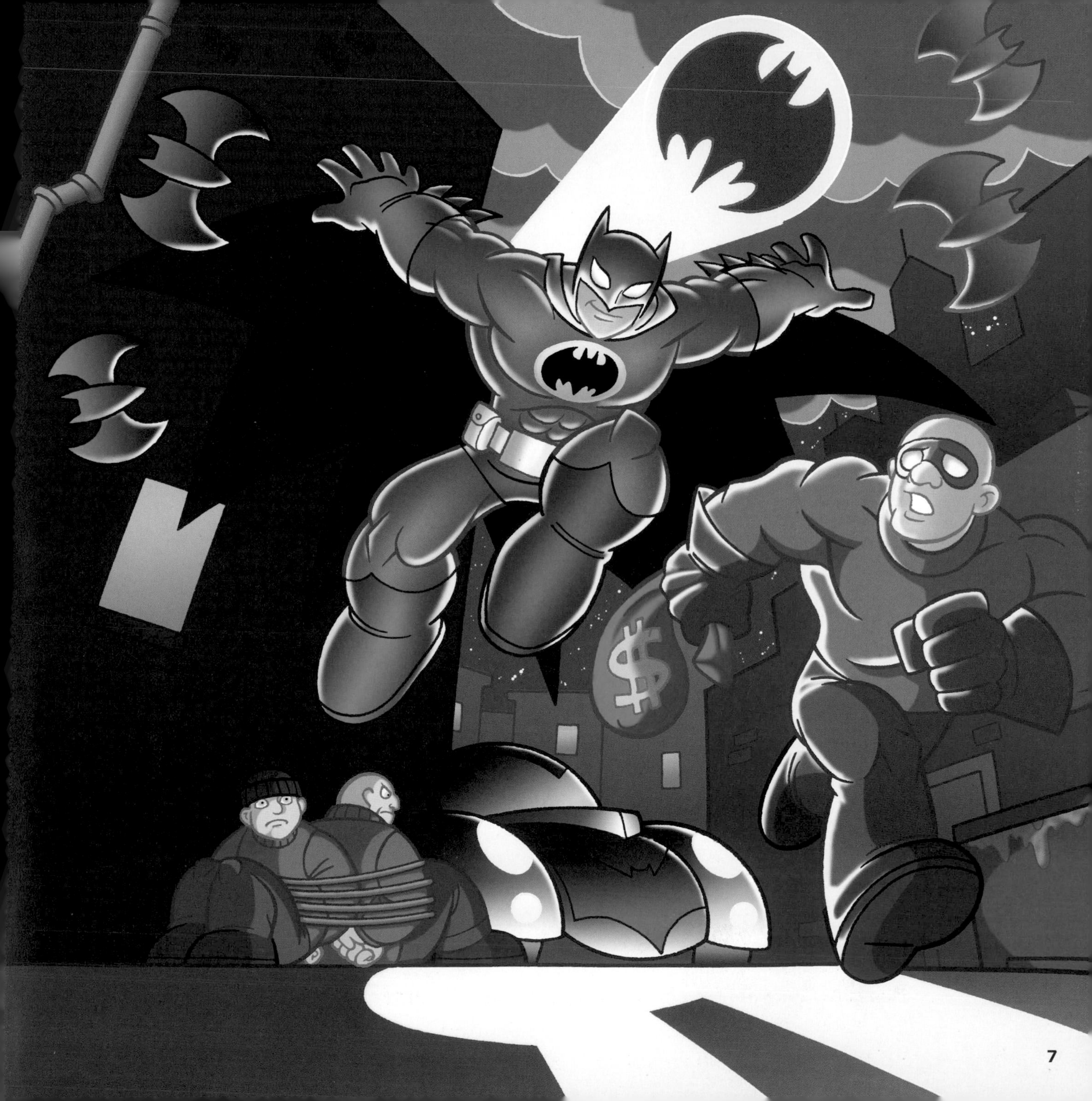

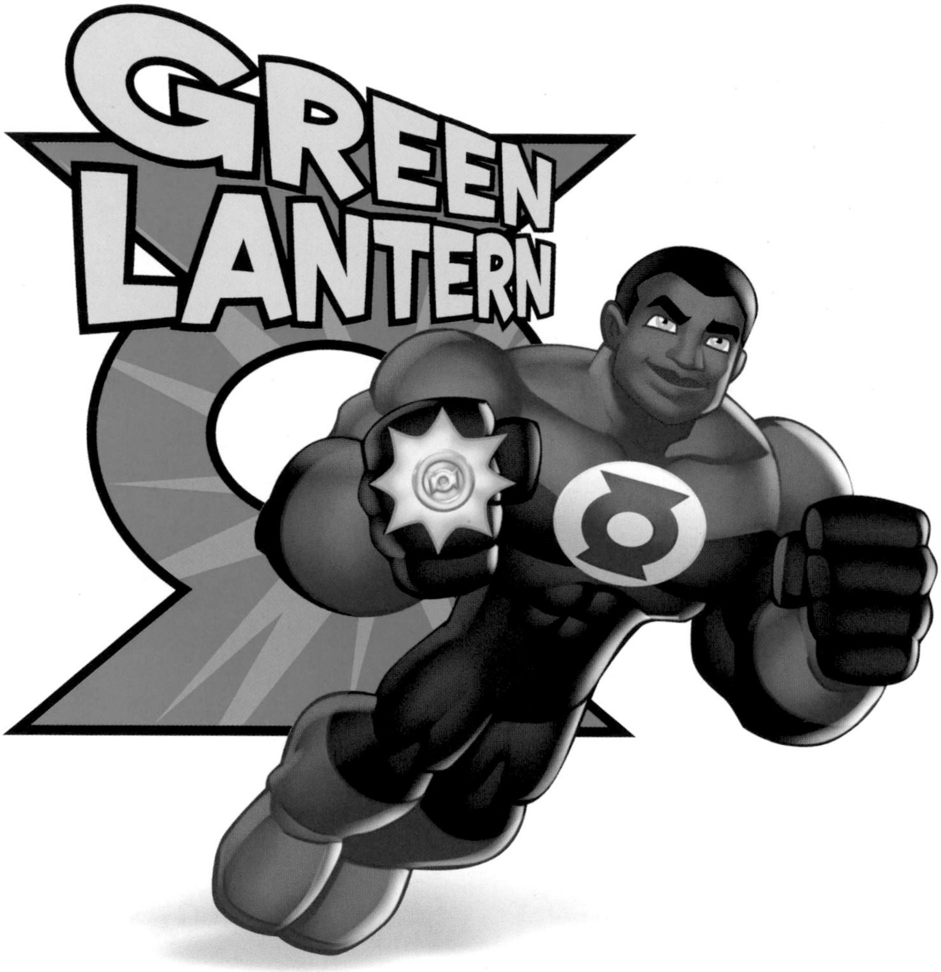
GREEN LANTERN

Green Lantern is a Guardian of the Galaxy. With his glowing green power ring, he can create anything that he can imagine—from unbreakable force fields and laser blasts to baseball bats and giant hands. It's Green Lantern's job to protect Earth from the dangers that come from outer space!

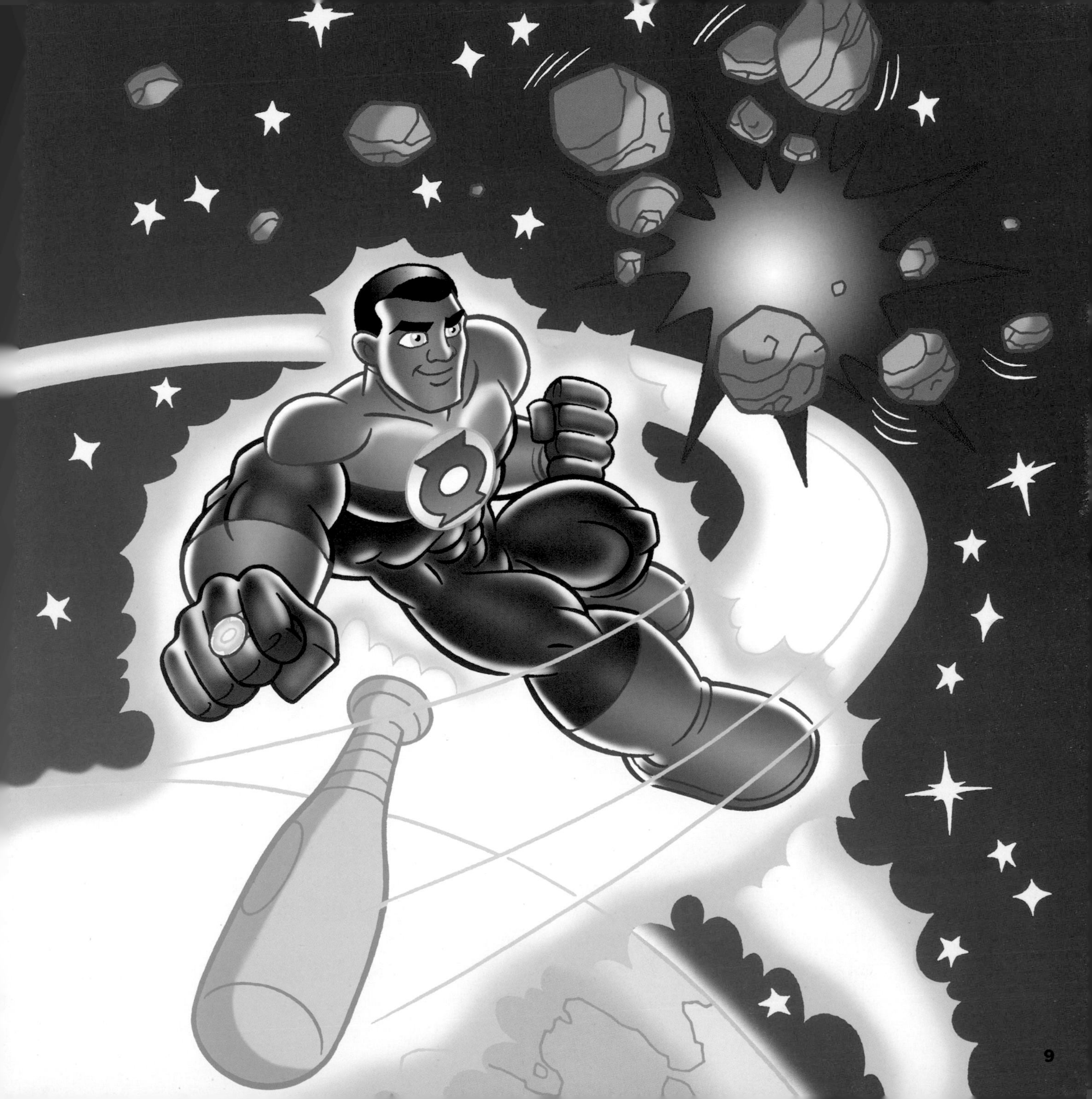

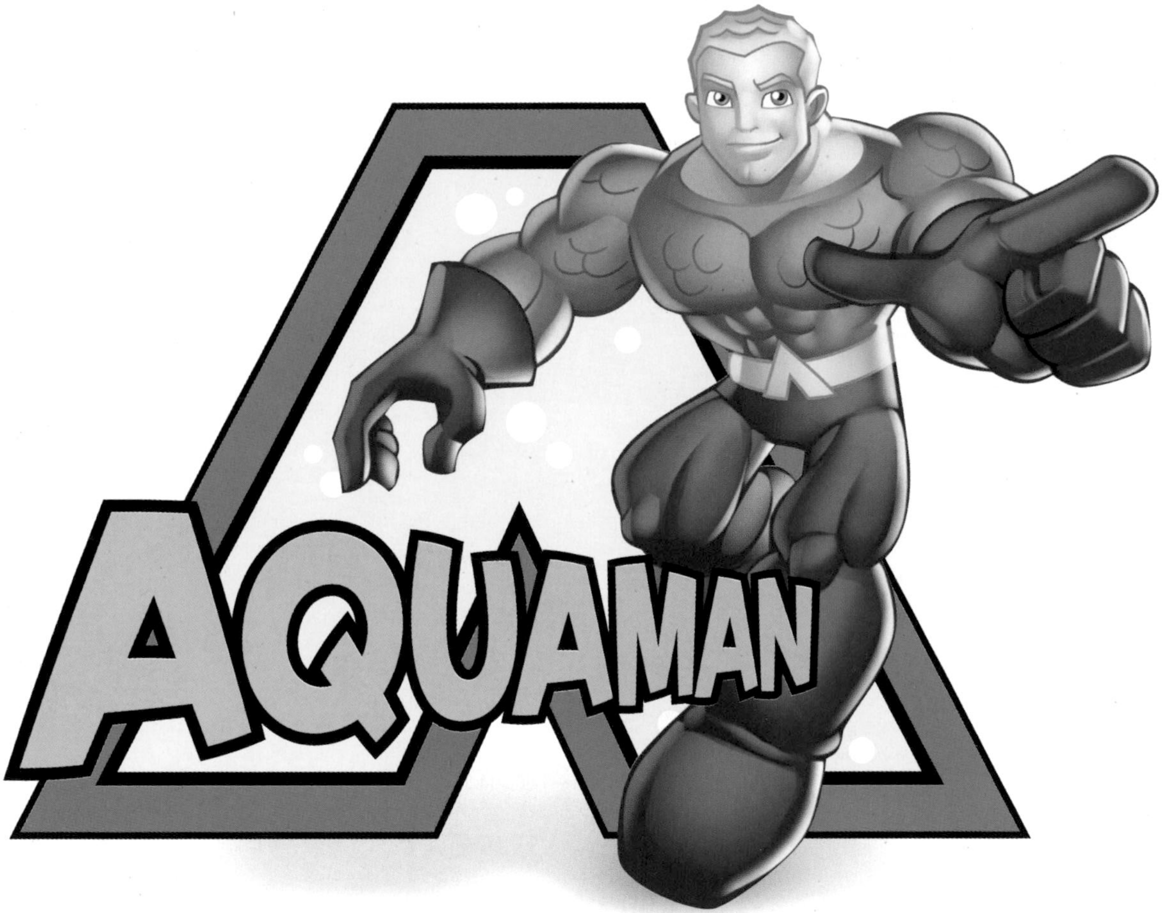
AQUAMAN

Aquaman is King of the Seven Seas and ruler of Atlantis, the legendary city beneath the ocean. He can breathe underwater and talk to all the creatures of the sea. They help Aquaman protect life in and out of the water. When Aquaman makes a big splash, he leaves bad guys all wet!

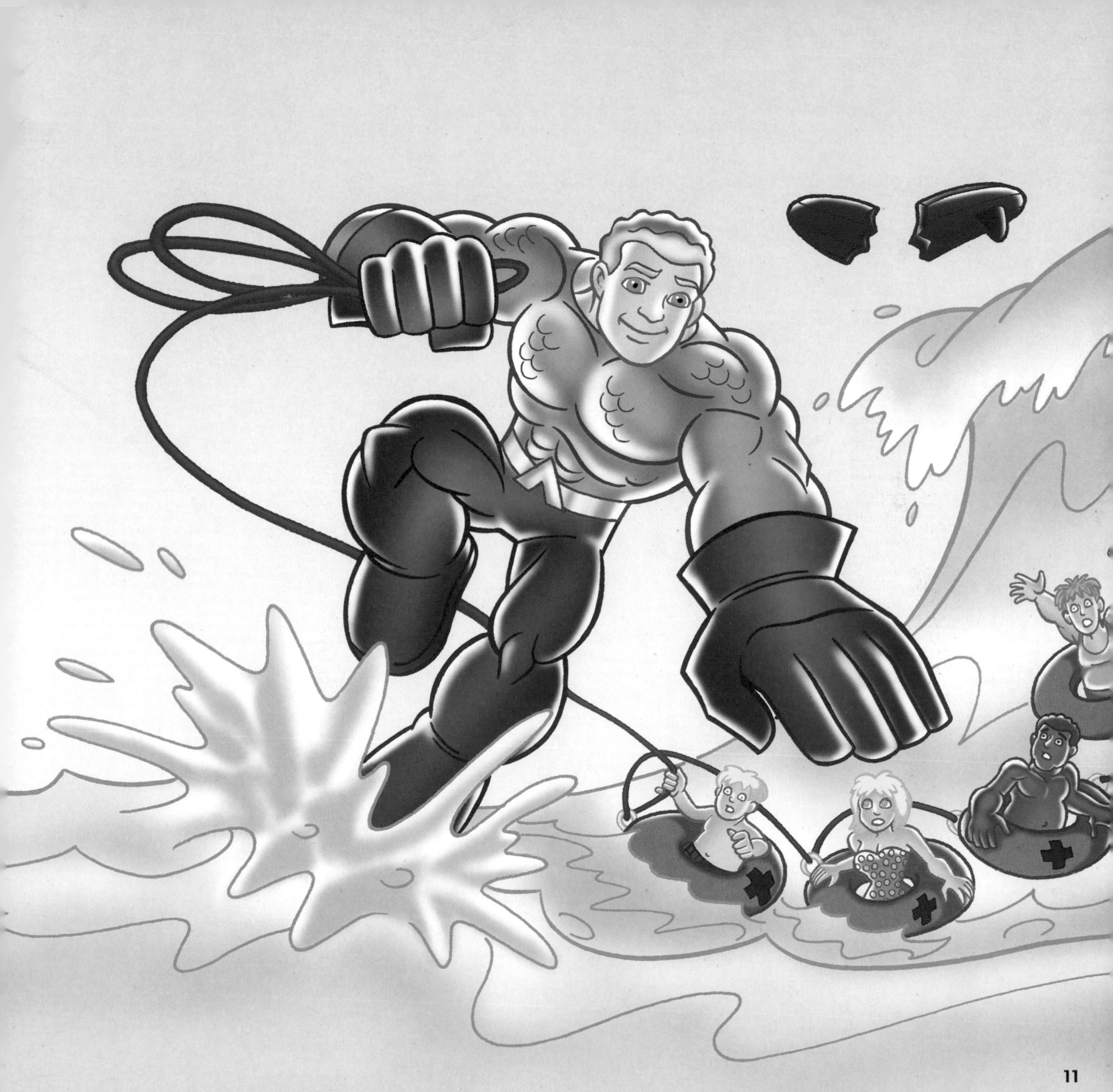

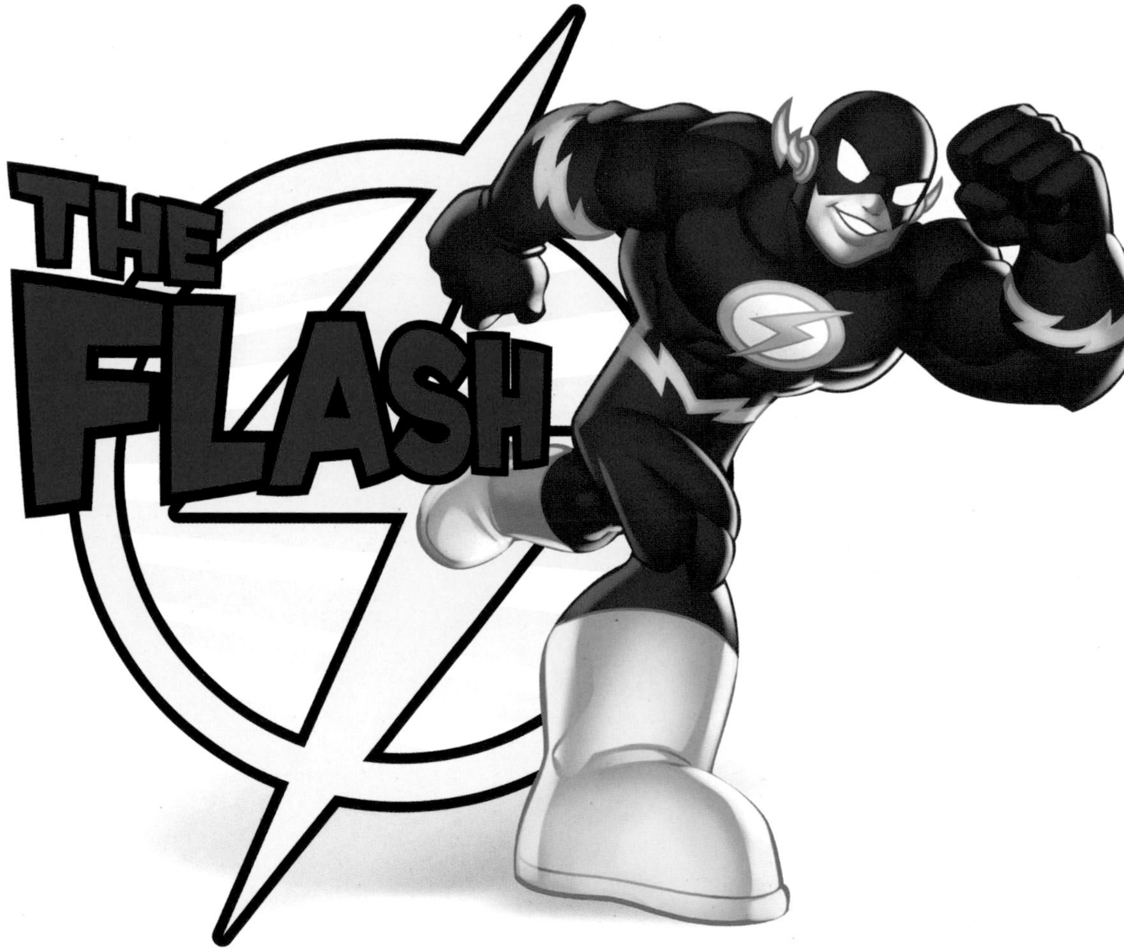
THE FLASH

The Flash is the Fastest Man Alive. He's so fast that he can run up walls and across water. He's even able to vibrate through solid objects so that he doesn't have to go around them when he's running at top speed. Now, that's fast! If bad guys even blink, it's too late—the Flash will catch them, quick as lightning!

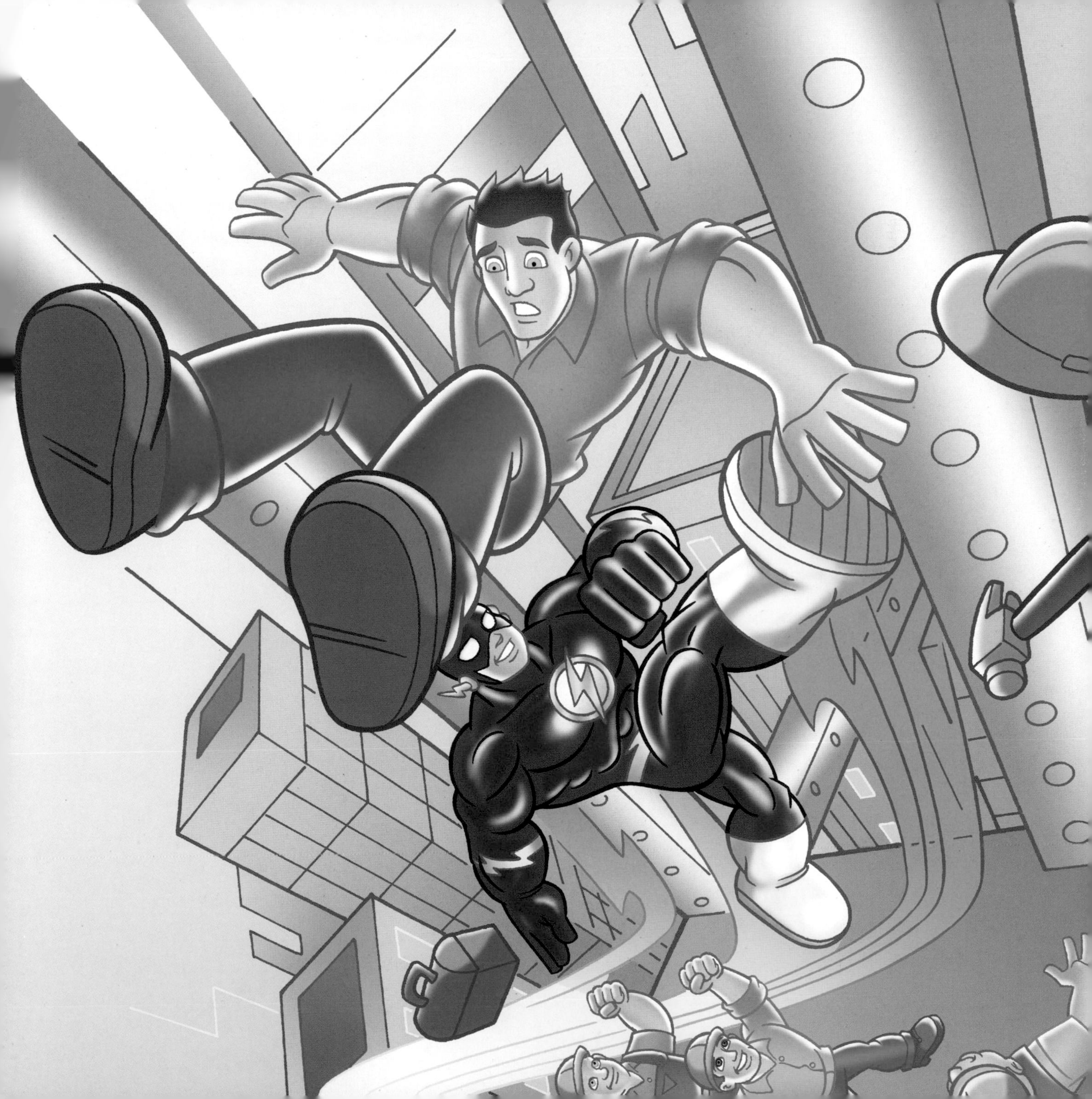

Using teamwork, Superman, Batman, Green Lantern, Aquaman, and the Flash combine their amazing skills and superpowers . . .

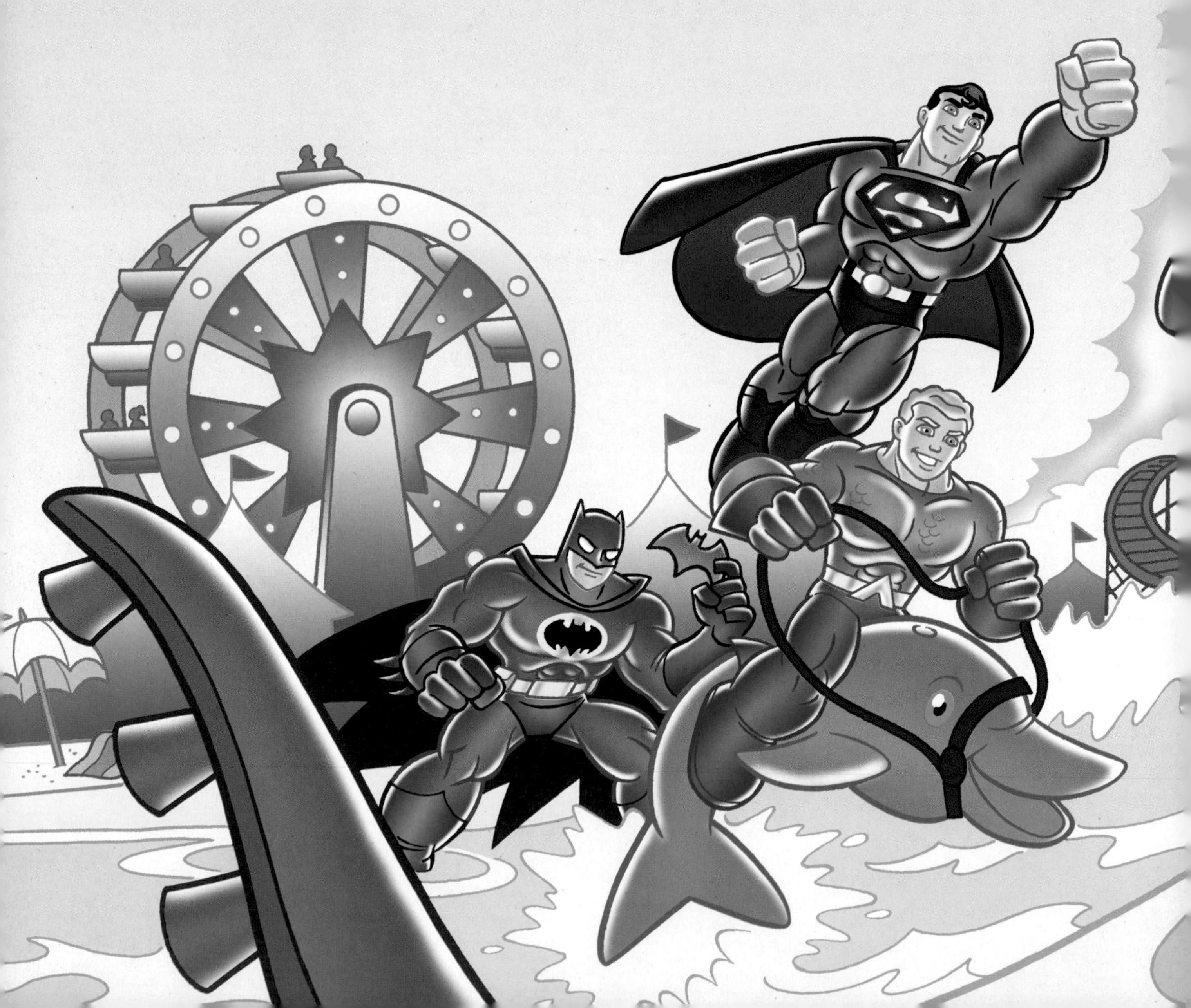

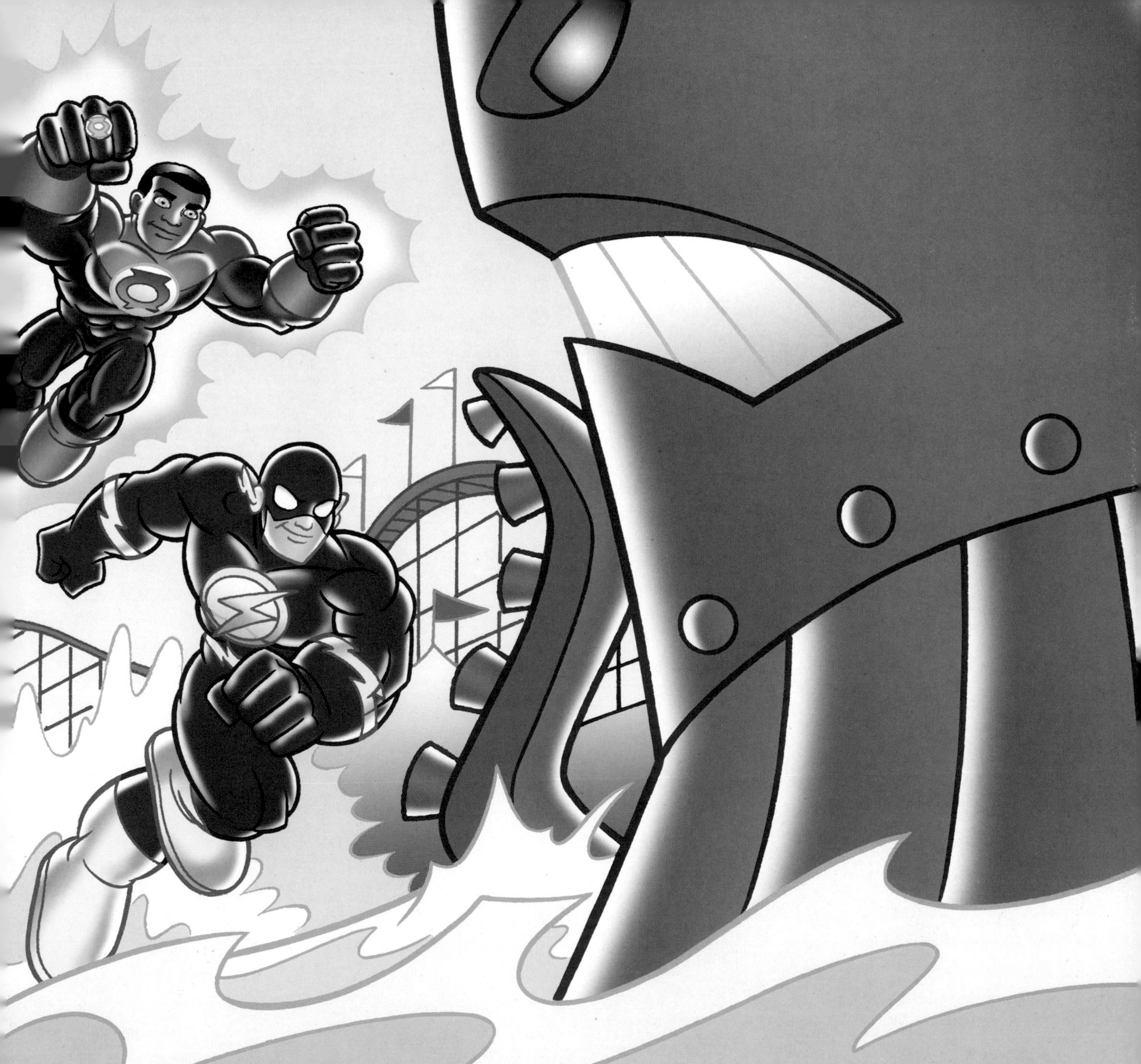

. . . to meet any challenge and face any danger, no matter how great. They are . . . **the Super Friends!**

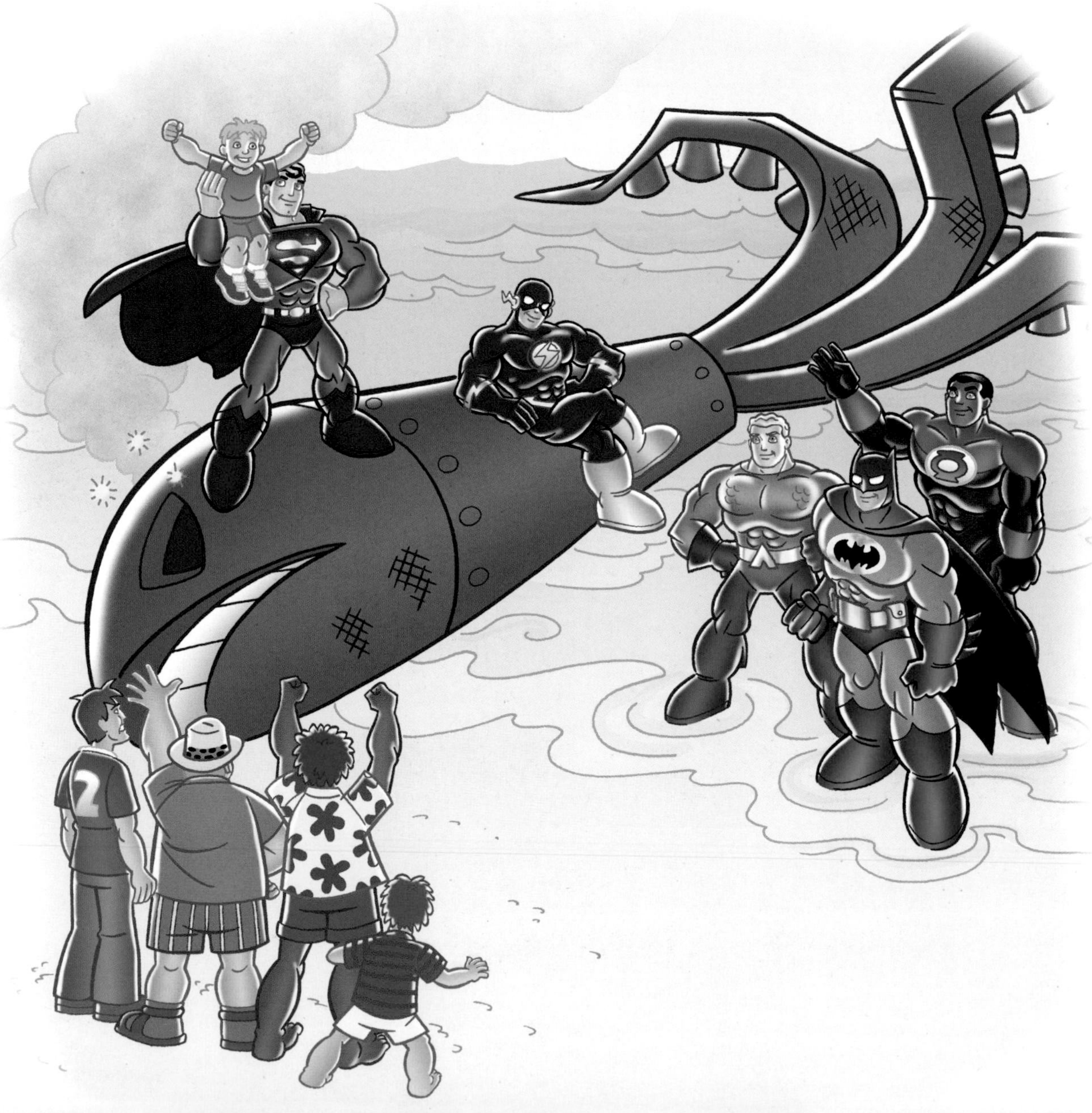

Battle in Space!

By Billy Wrecks

Illustrated by Erik Doescher and Elisa Marrucchi

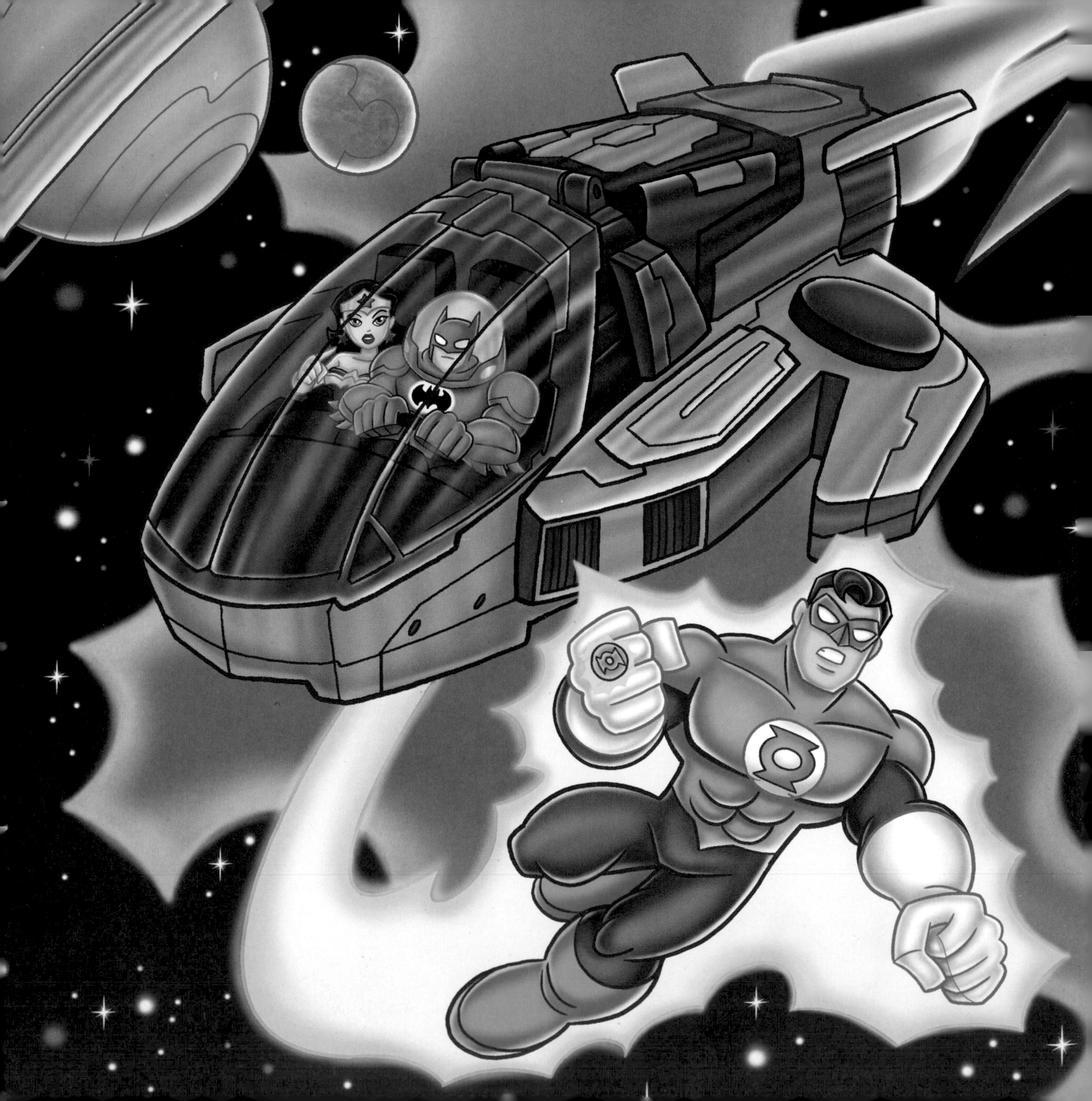

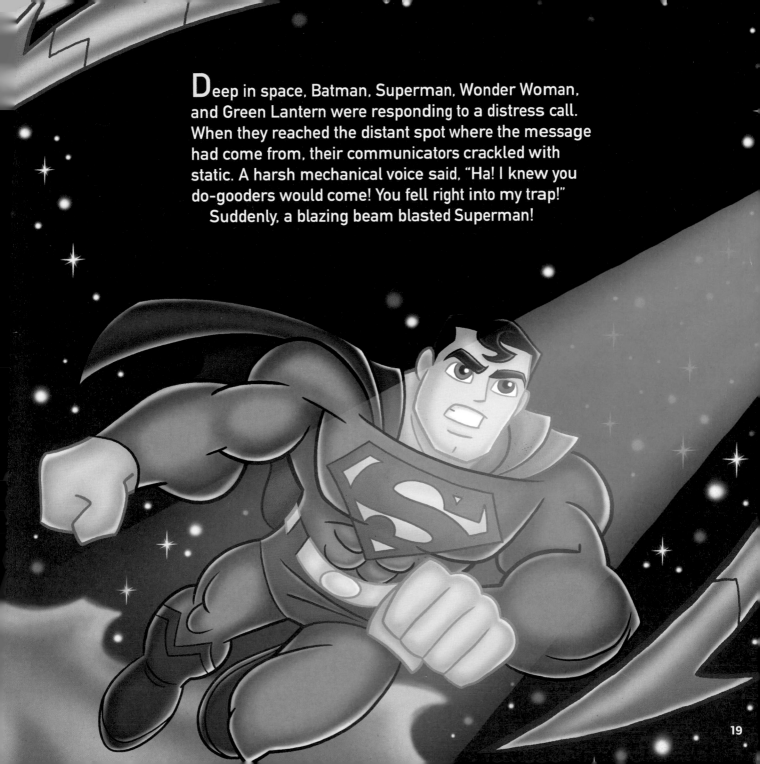

Deep in space, Batman, Superman, Wonder Woman, and Green Lantern were responding to a distress call. When they reached the distant spot where the message had come from, their communicators crackled with static. A harsh mechanical voice said, "Ha! I knew you do-gooders would come! You fell right into my trap!"

Suddenly, a blazing beam blasted Superman!

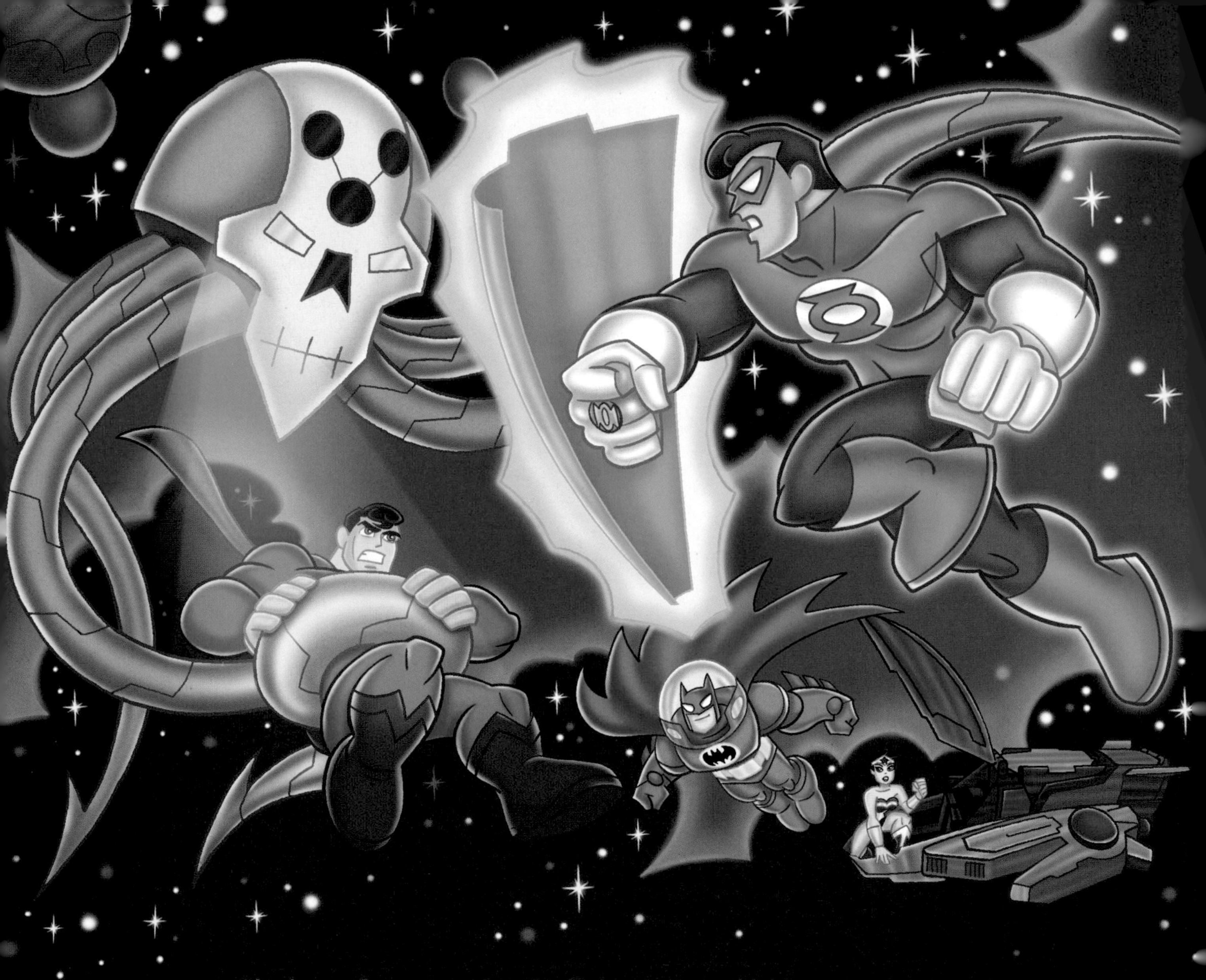

"And now Superman is mine!" the villain said, his spaceship coming into view. "Even the mighty Superman is no match for the amazing mind of **BRAINIAC**. He will make an excellent addition to my collection of unique beings."

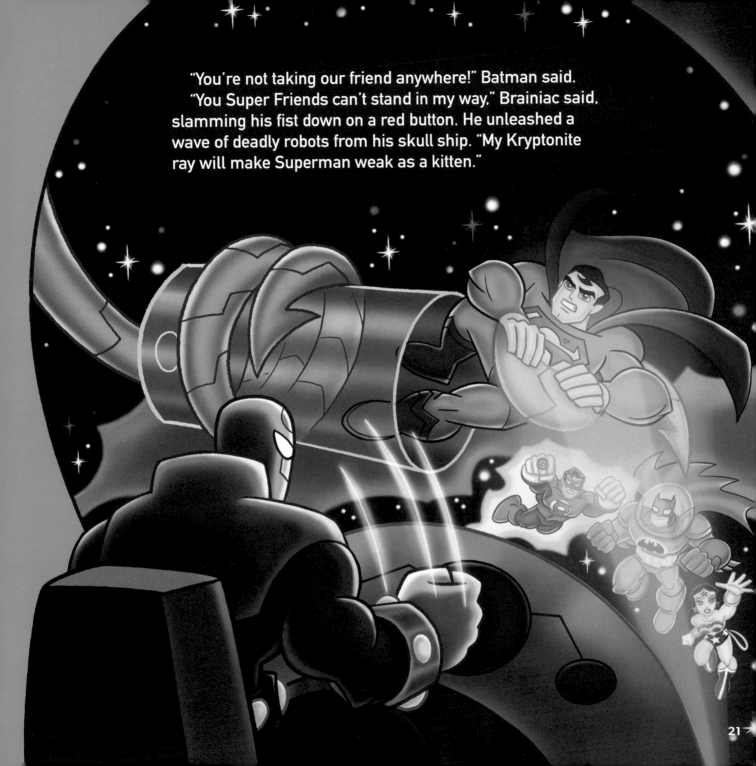

"You're not taking our friend anywhere!" Batman said.
"You Super Friends can't stand in my way," Brainiac said,
slamming his fist down on a red button. He unleashed a
wave of deadly robots from his skull ship. "My Kryptonite
ray will make Superman weak as a kitten."

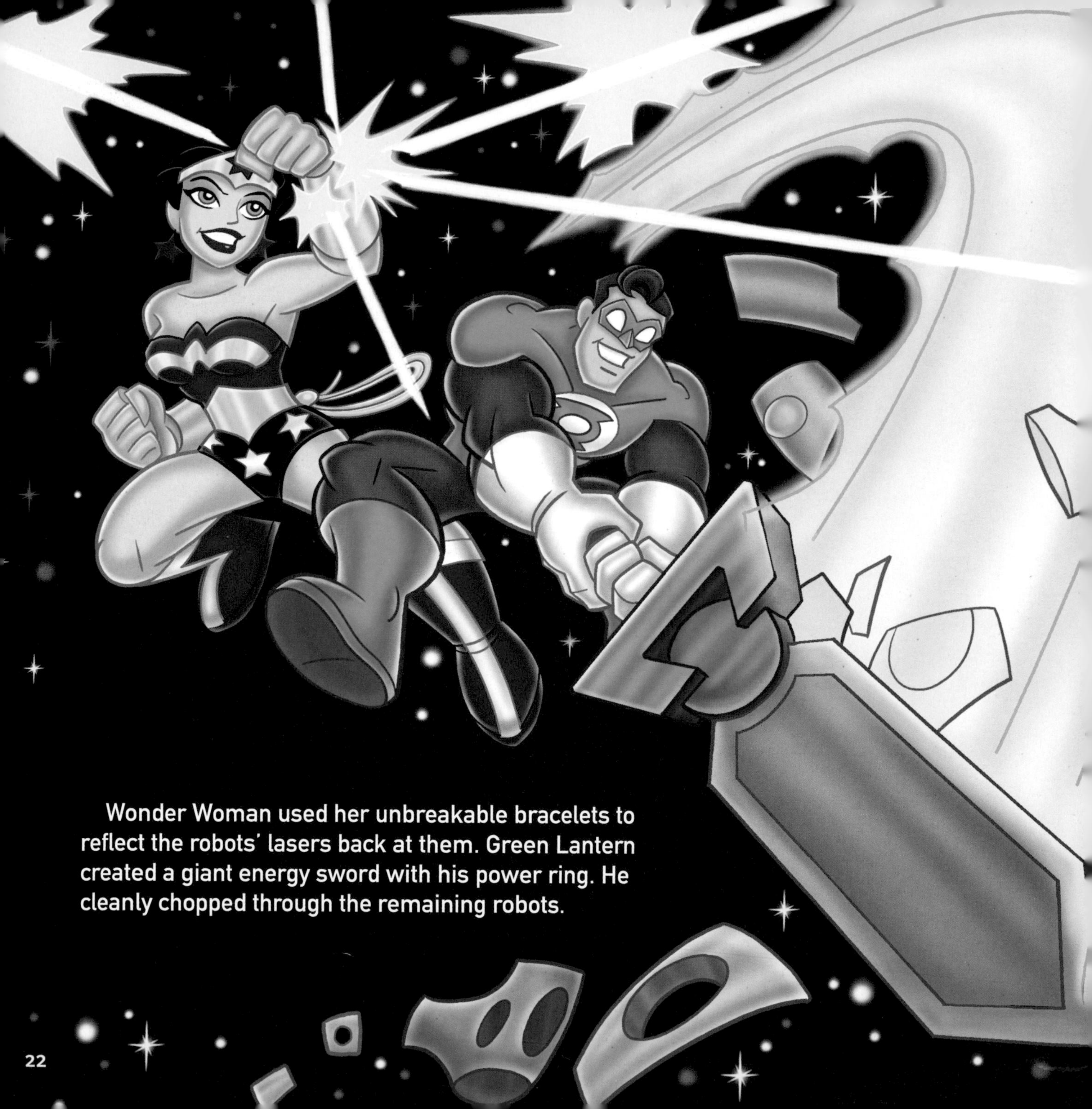

Wonder Woman used her unbreakable bracelets to reflect the robots' lasers back at them. Green Lantern created a giant energy sword with his power ring. He cleanly chopped through the remaining robots.

Using his jet pack, Batman rocketed to Brainiac's ship. He was not about to let the villain get away with his friend. He snuck inside just as the ship roared into space at light speed.

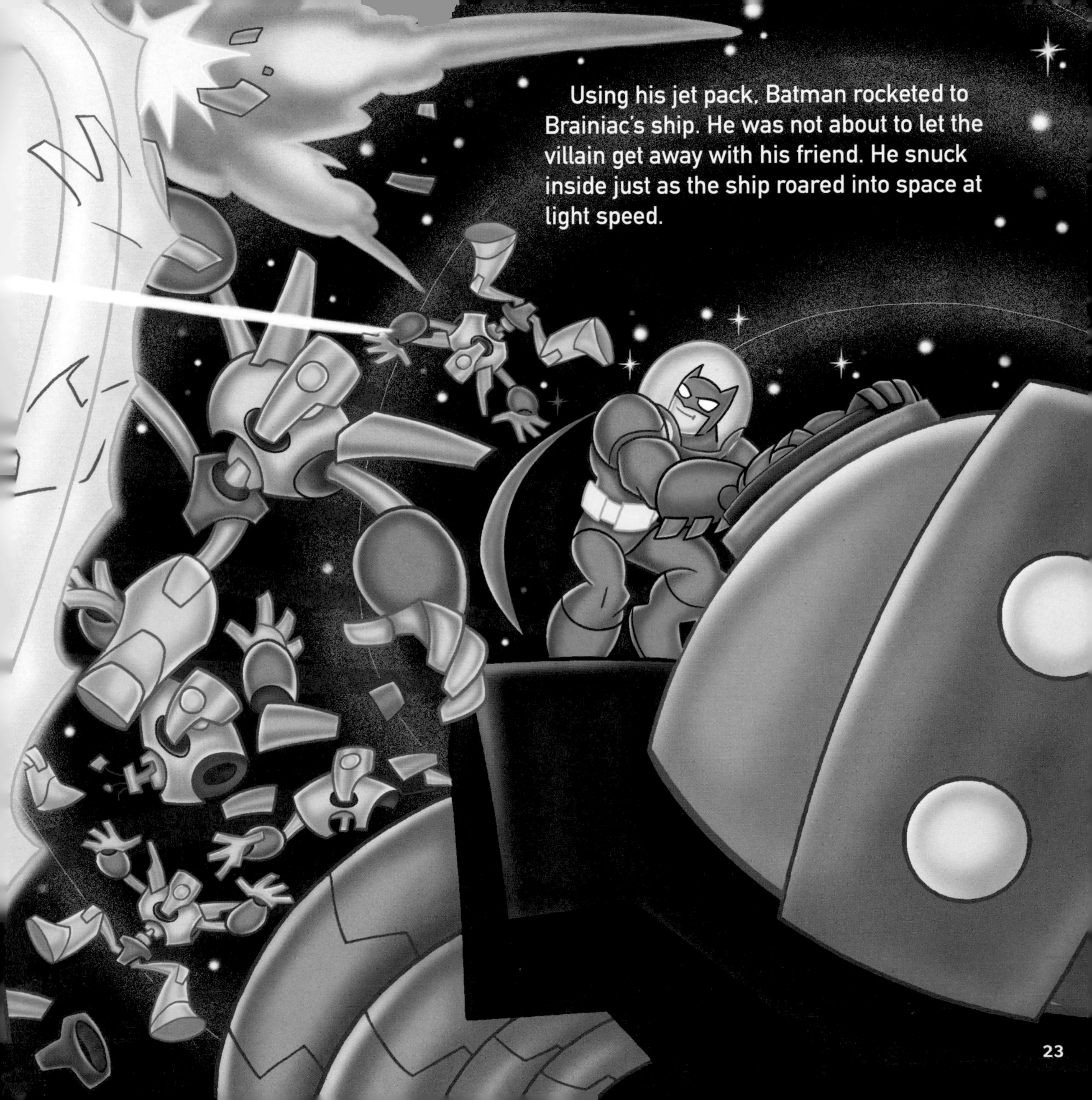

"Brainiac is getting away!" Wonder Woman shouted.

"Not if I can help it," Green Lantern said. He used his power ring to bring Batman's drifting ship over to them, and Wonder Woman jumped inside.

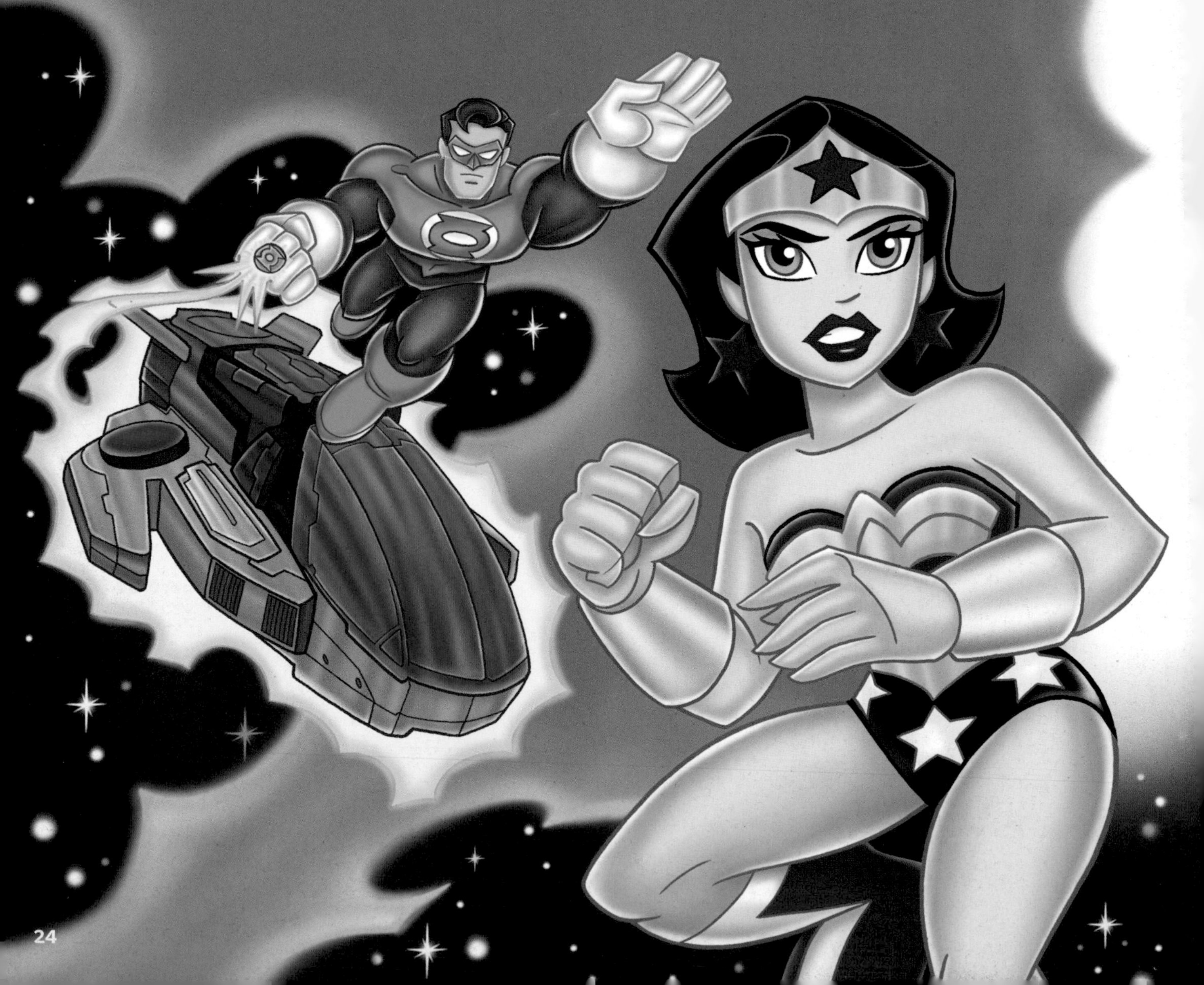

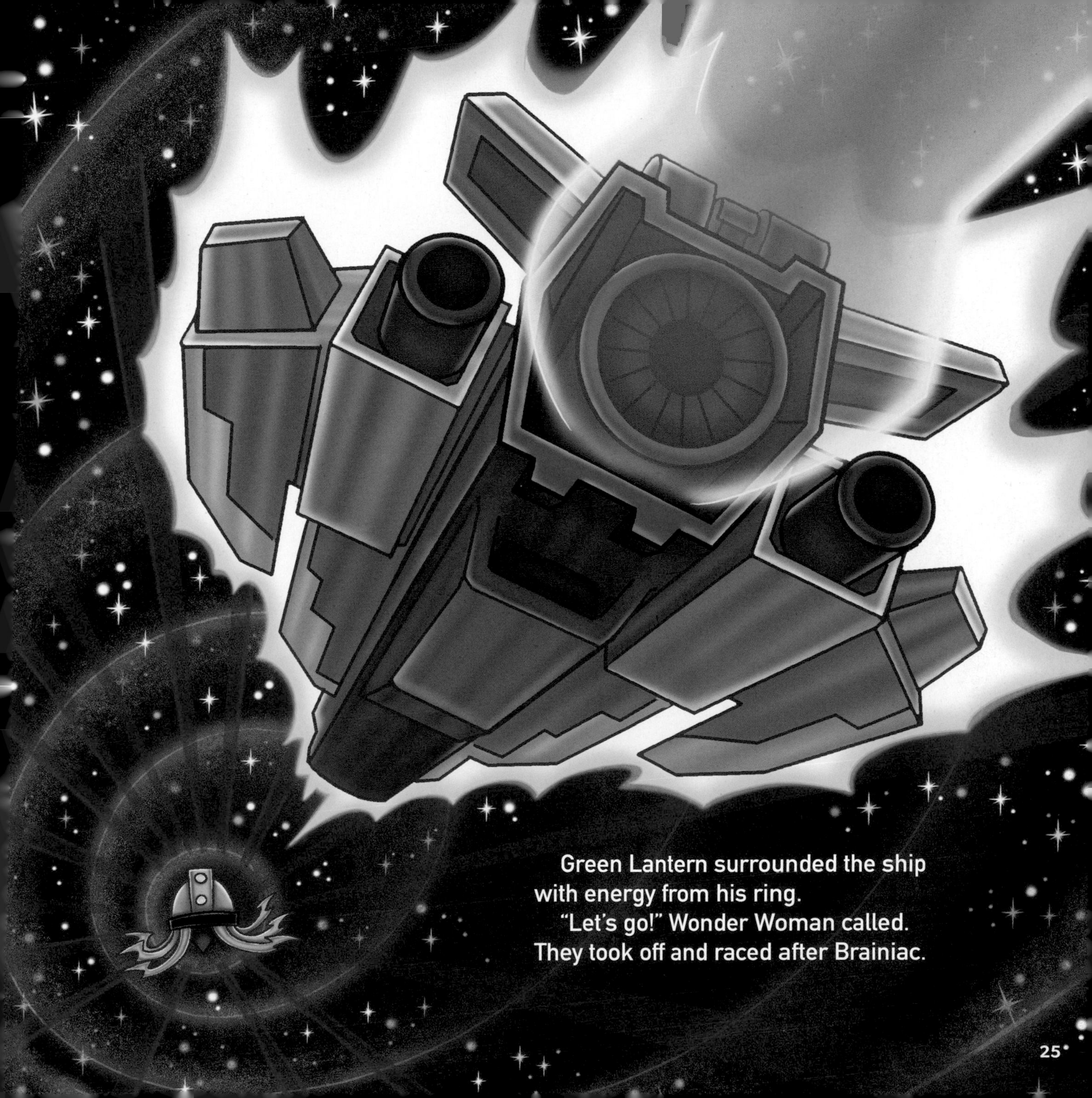

Green Lantern surrounded the ship with energy from his ring.

"Let's go!" Wonder Woman called. They took off and raced after Brainiac.

“When I want something, I get it,” Brainiac told Superman. “And now I have *you*.”

“Just wait until my friends get here,” Superman replied.

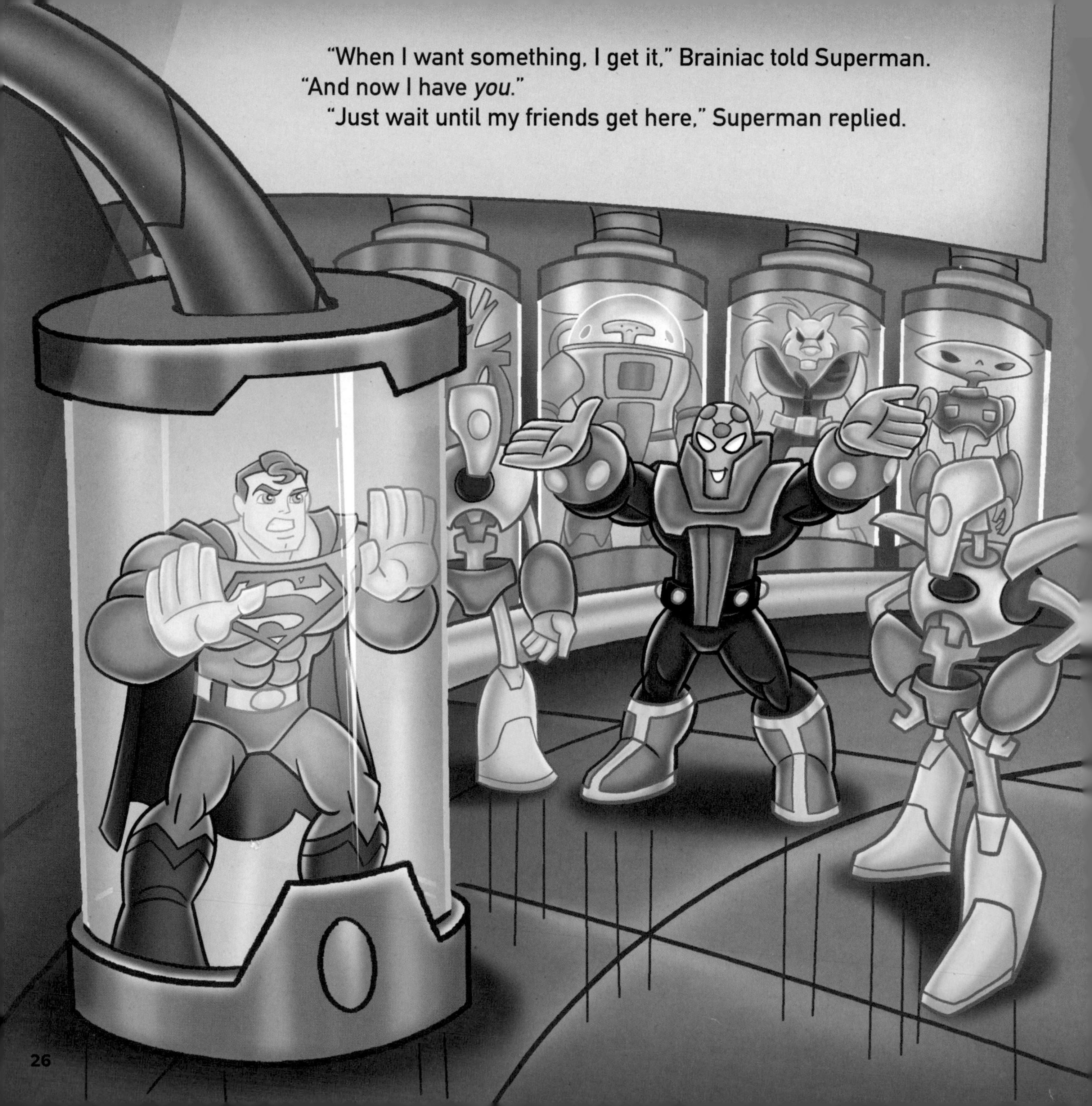

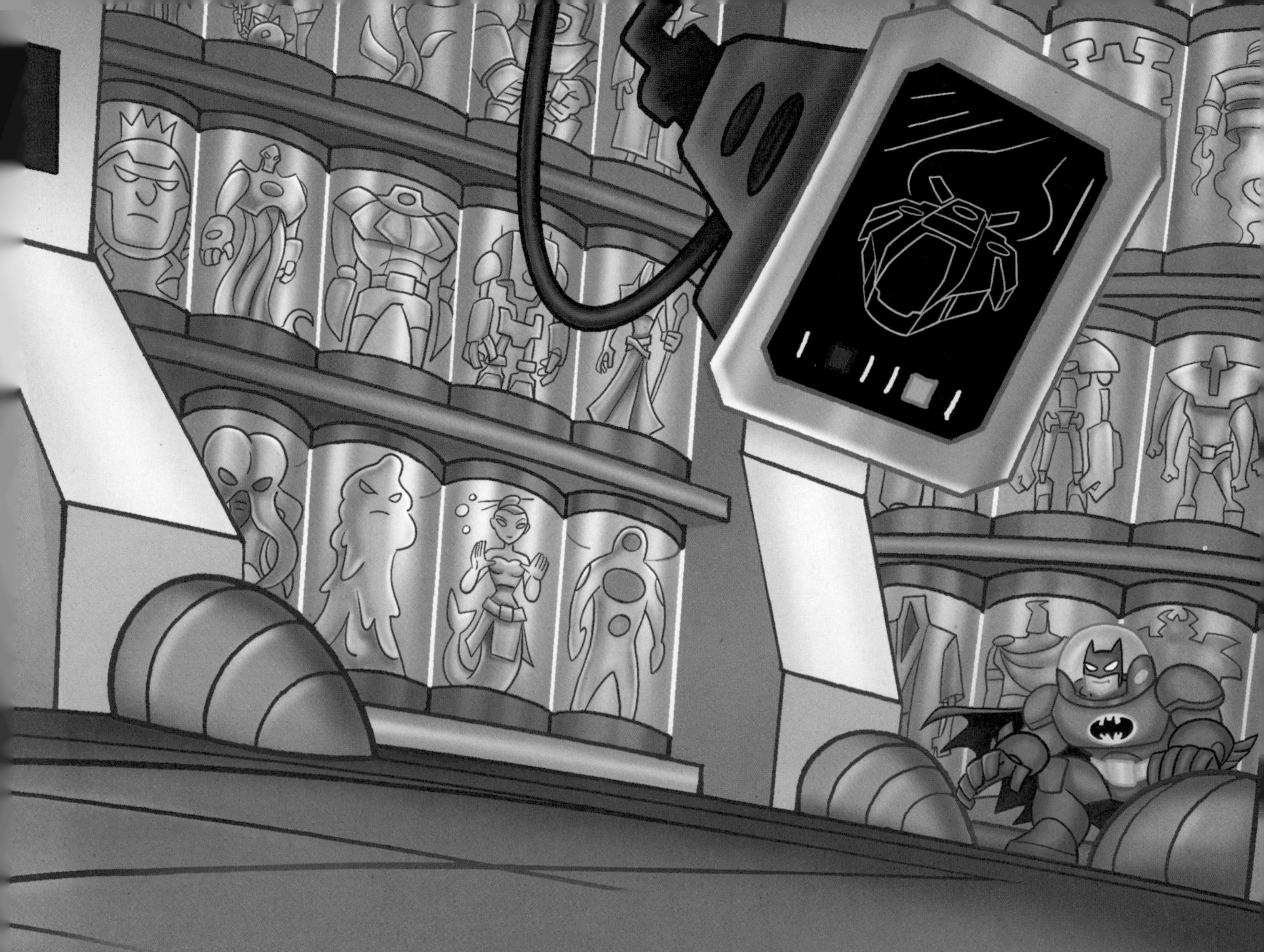

"We have left them far behind," Brainiac said. "They are of no concern."

But Brainiac could not have been more wrong. Batman was hiding in the shadows. Looking up, he saw the thousands of captives in Brainiac's ship. That gave him an idea.

When Wonder Woman and Green Lantern reached Brainiac's ship, they slipped through the airlock. An alarm sounded!

"What? The Super Friends?" Brainiac shouted.

The heroes dashed onto the bridge and began to fight the villain's robots. But there were too many of them!

"Did you two really think you could stop me?" Brainiac laughed.

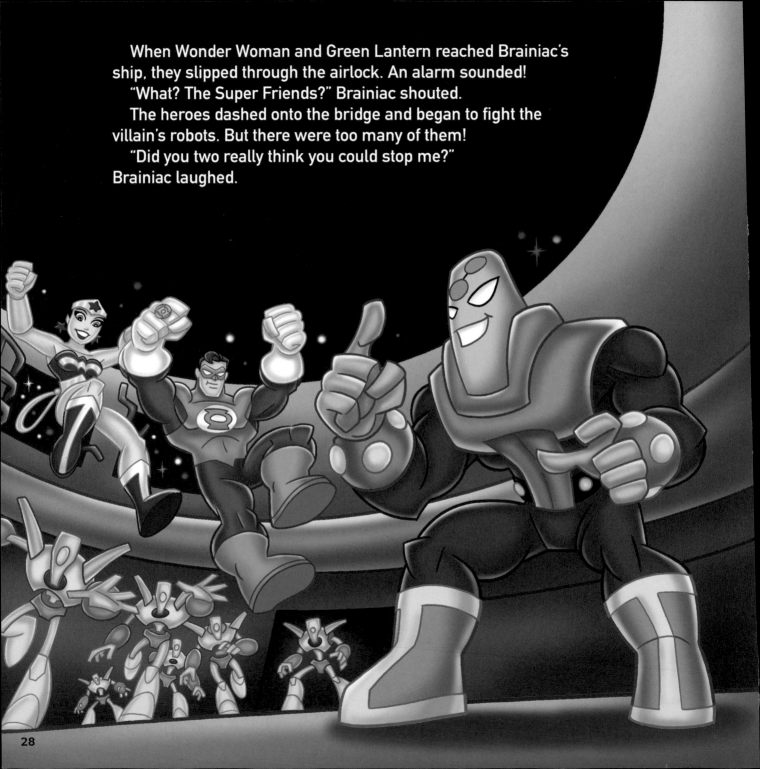

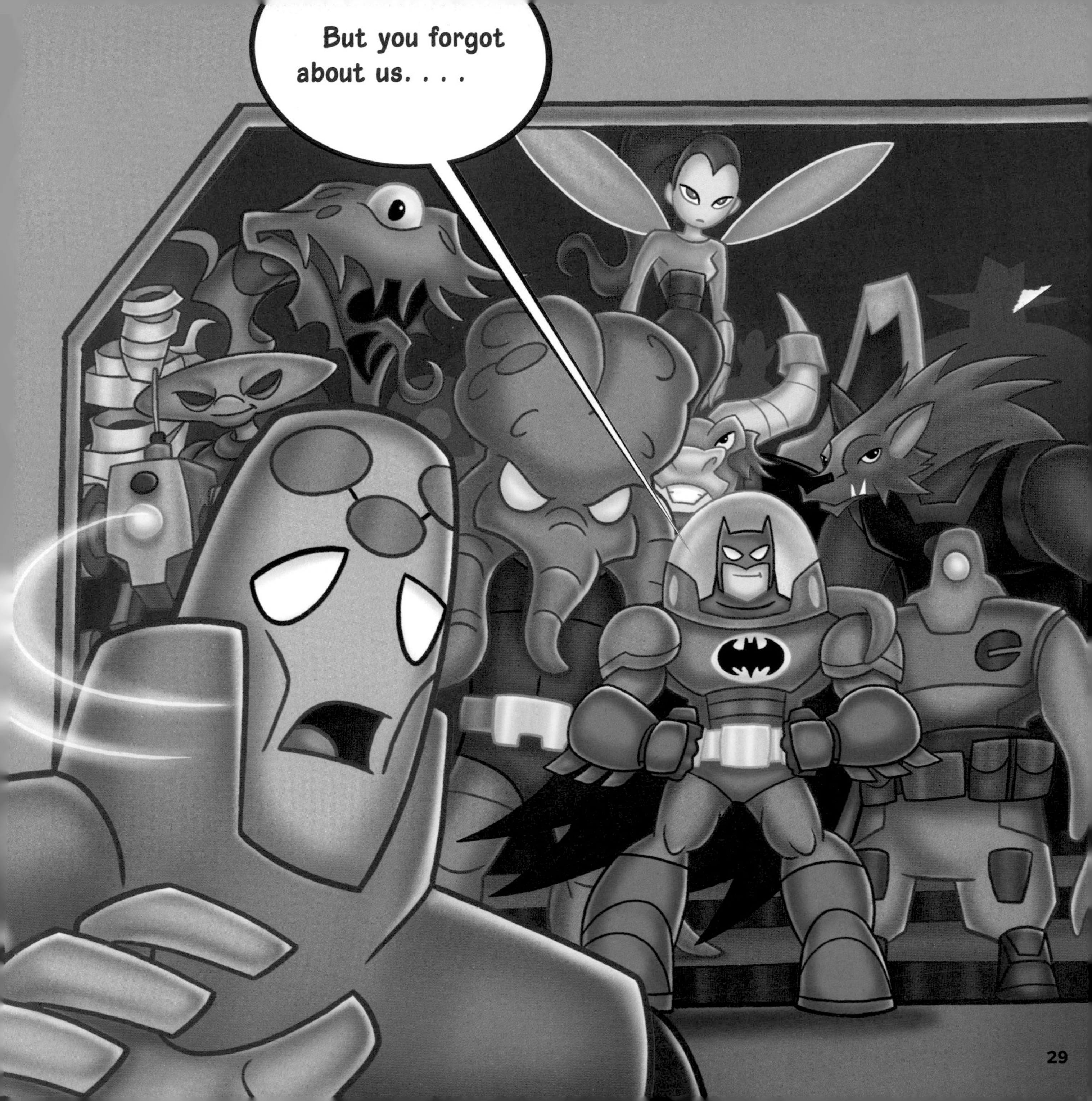
But you forgot about us. . . .

Batman had released all the aliens Brainiac had collected from across the universe. They were happy to help bring Brainiac to justice. After smashing his robots, they chased Brainiac toward Wonder Woman—who was waiting for him with her magic lasso.

Green Lantern crushed the Kryptonite ray and freed Superman.

"Thanks!" Superman said, quickly regaining his full strength.

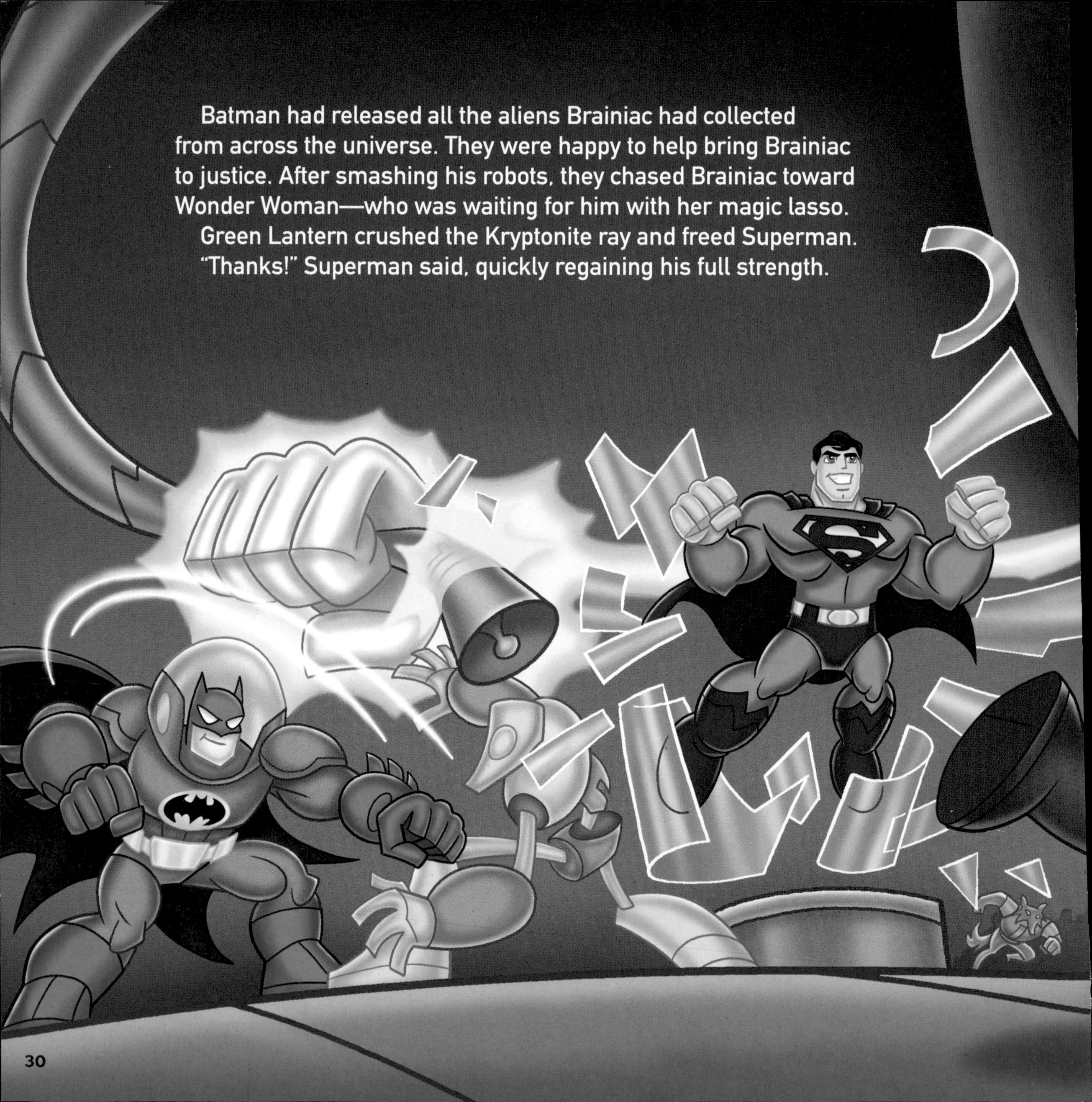

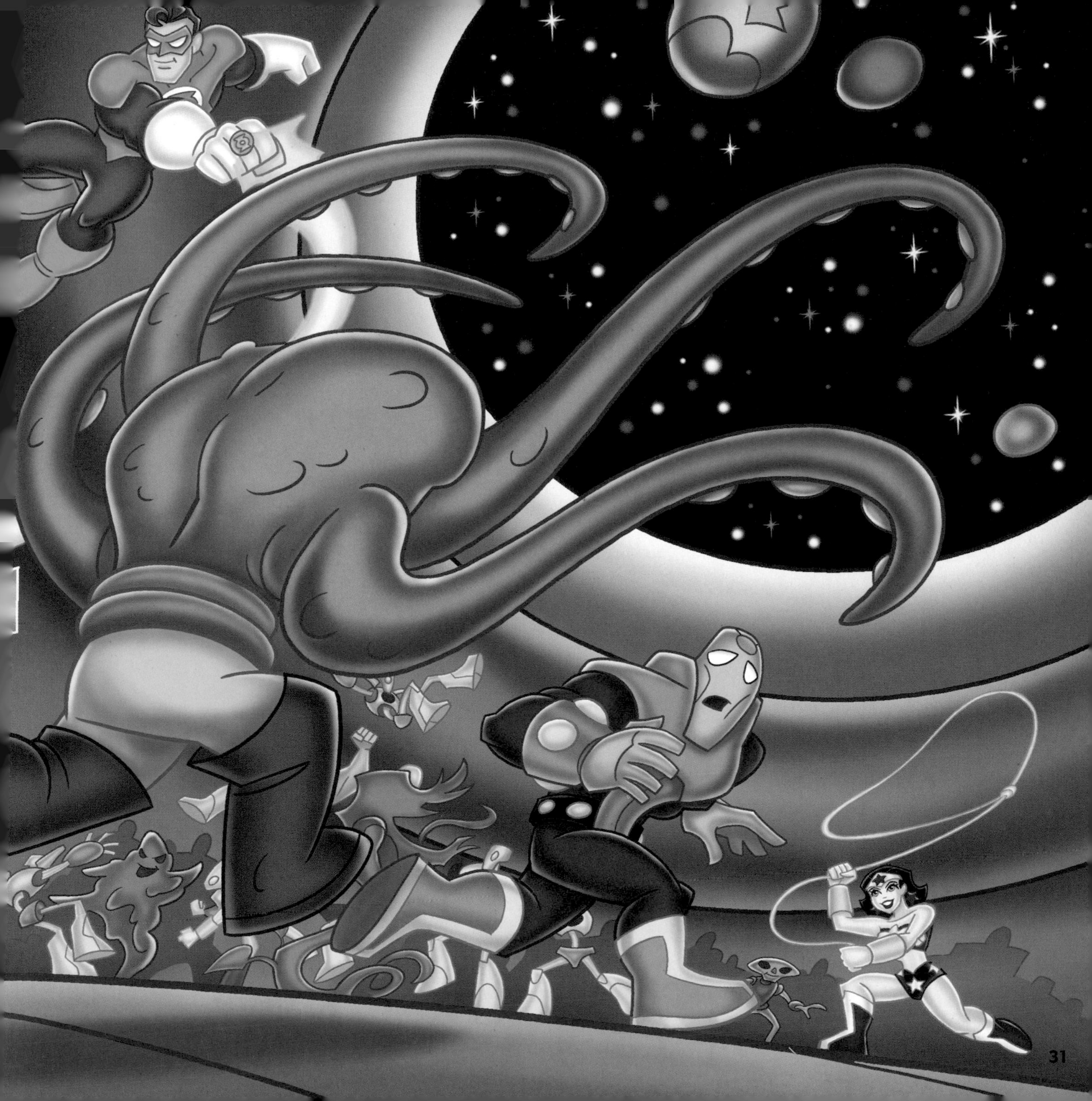

"This ship will get you home," Green Lantern told the aliens.

"And it will get *you* to the intergalactic authorities," Wonder Woman said to Brainiac, who was now a prisoner in one of his own cells.

Batman added, "Brainiac wasn't smart enough to know that when you mess with one of the Super Friends . . ."

"... you're messing with *all* of the Super Friends," Superman finished.

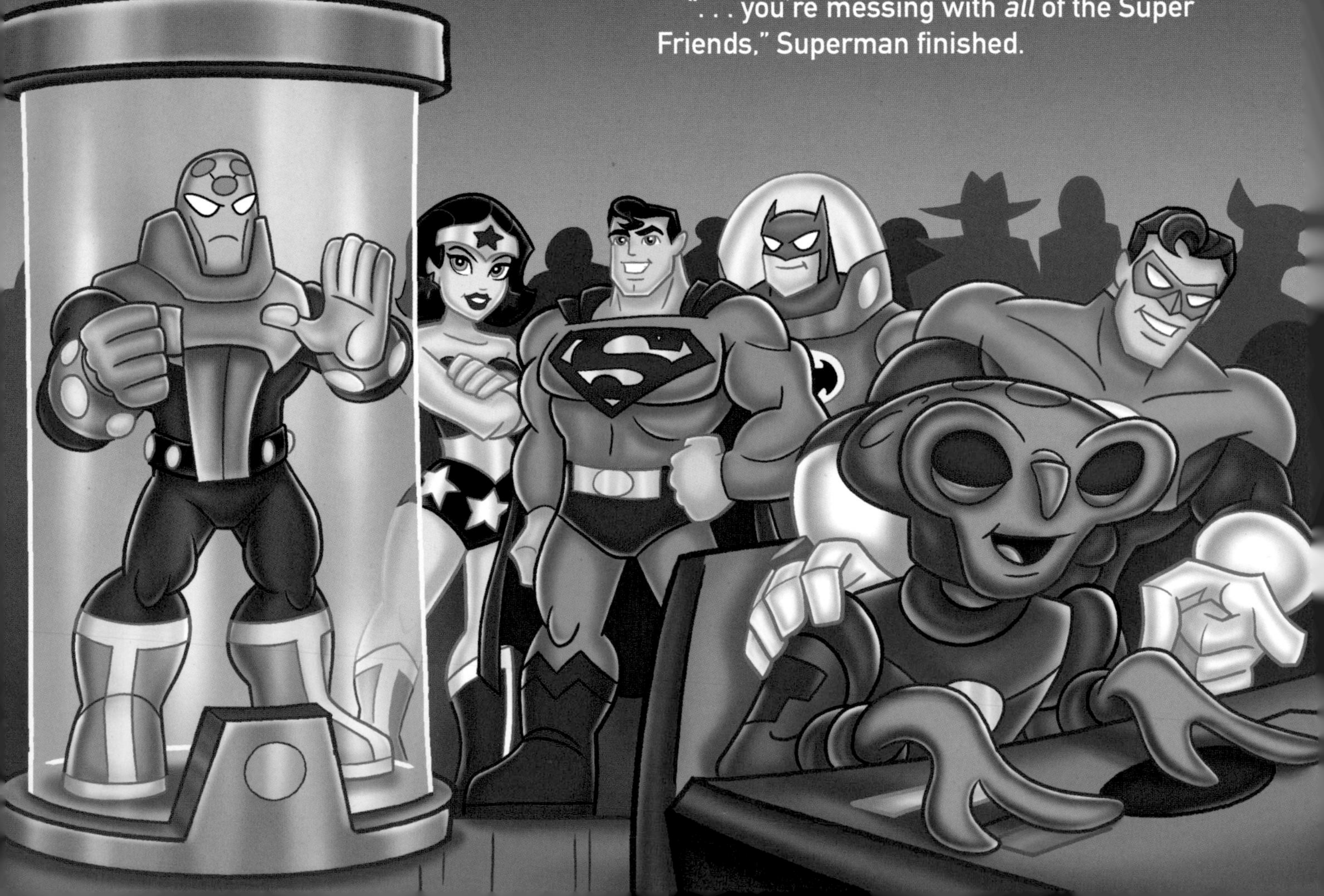

DC SUPER FRIENDS™

JAILBREAK!

By Billy Wrecks

Illustrated by Francesco Legramandi

At a maximum-security jail in Metropolis, the super-villains Clayface, Mr. Freeze, and Black Manta were kept behind bars. Nobody wanted these bad guys running free and committing crimes.

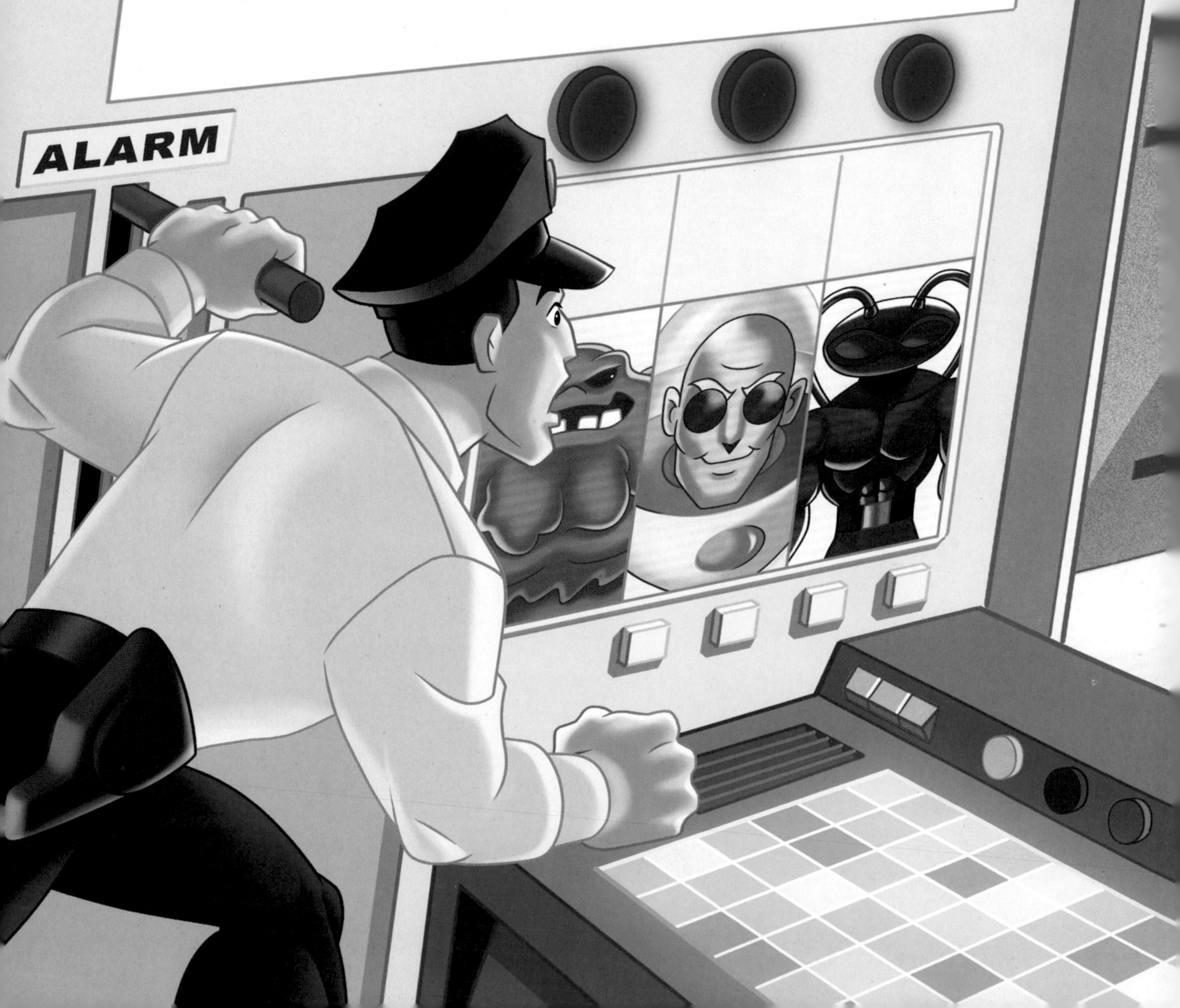
ALARM

Everything was quiet, when suddenly there was an explosion. "Jailbreak!" a guard yelled, pulling the alarm.

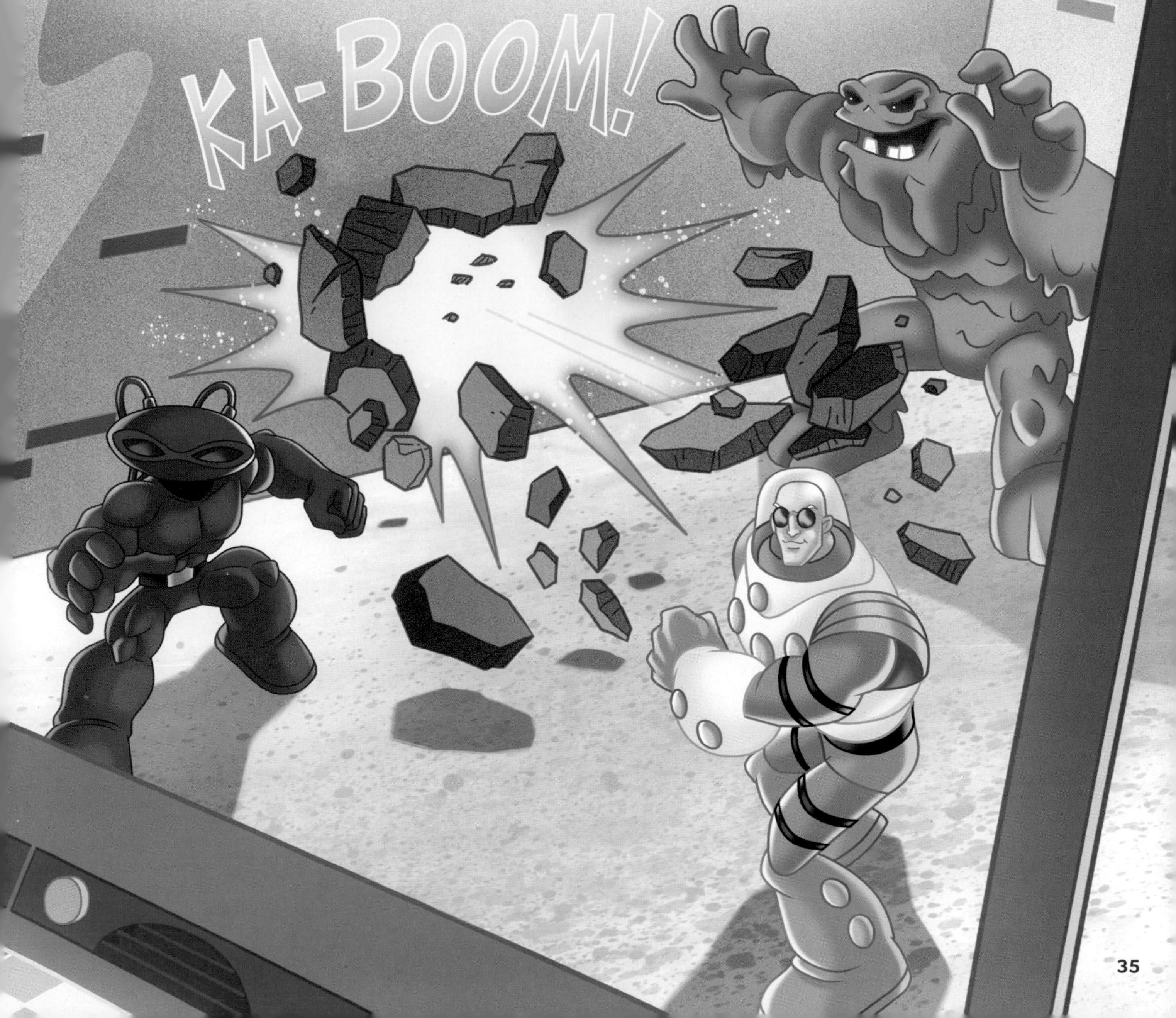
KA-BOOM!

"Hey, it's the Joker!" Clayface shouted as the bad guys climbed through the hole in the prison wall.

"Gotham City has been so *boring* without you," the criminal clown said. "No bank robberies. No freeze rays. No sinking ships. No fun at all! I thought you three might like to help me have some laughs."

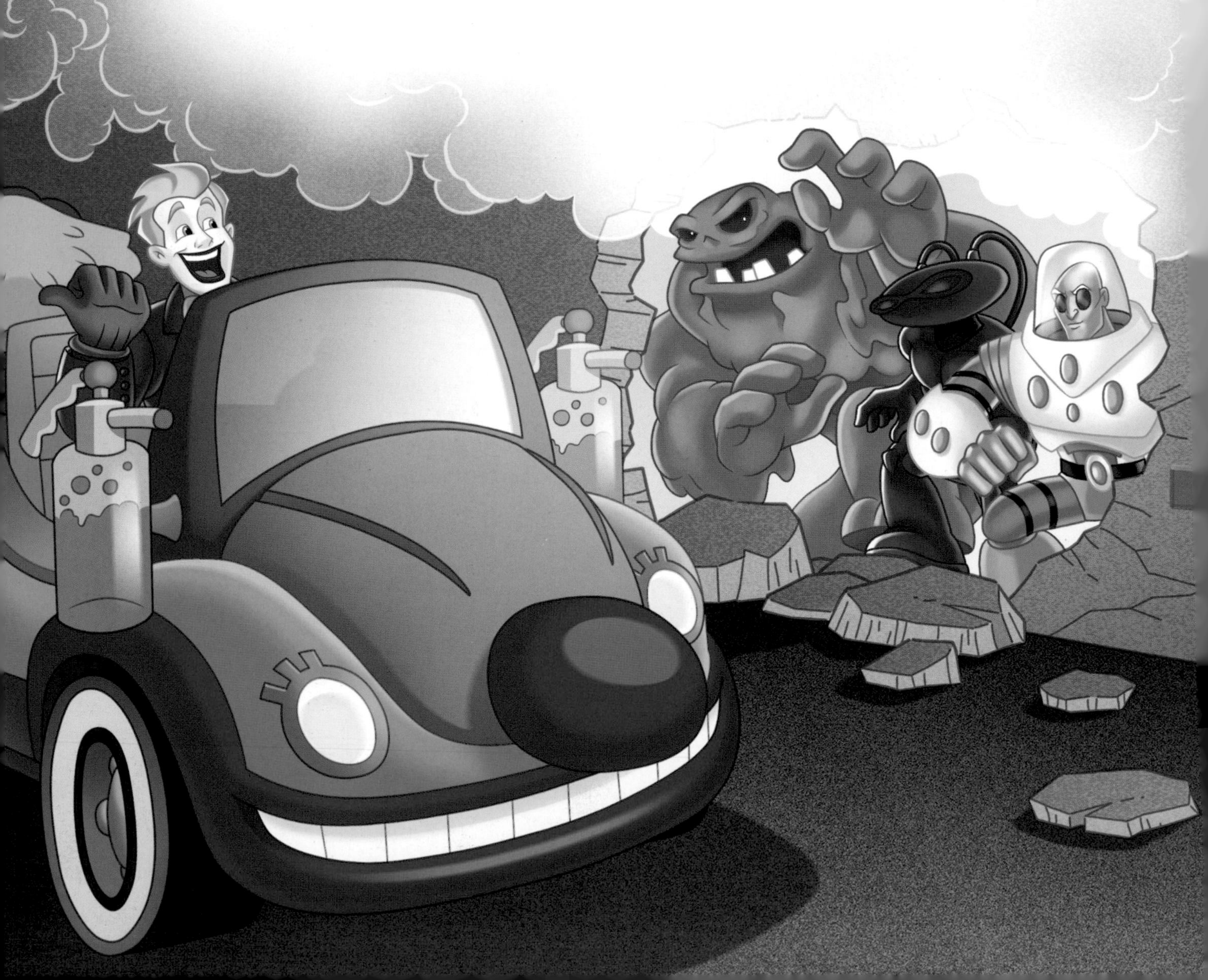

"Let's go!" the bad guys cheered, jumping into the Jokermobile. The Joker giggled and hit the gas. They took off down the road.

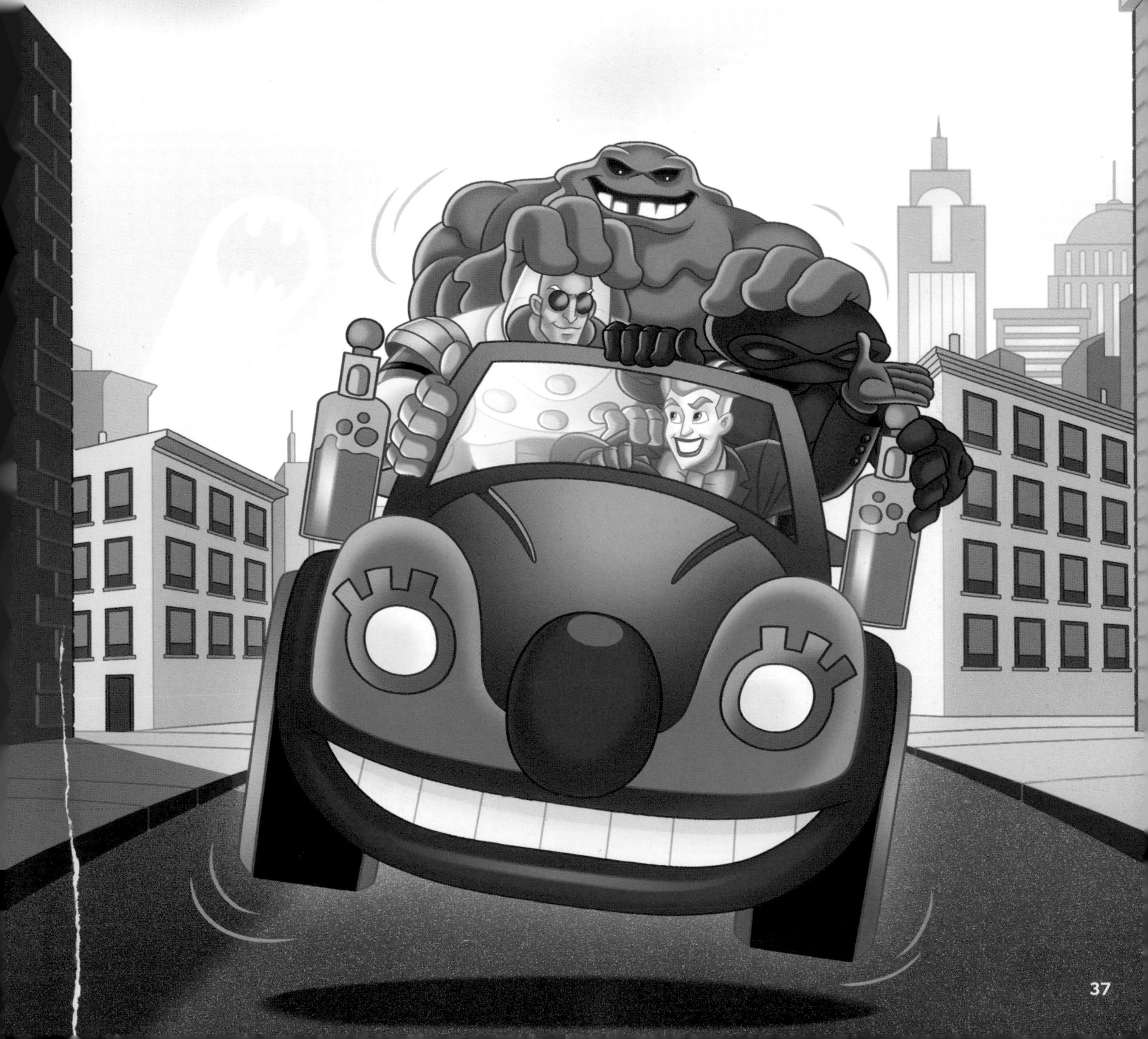

Batman saw the villains crashing into Gotham City.

"Super Friends," Batman said into his communicator, "the Joker and his friends have come to town to cause trouble."

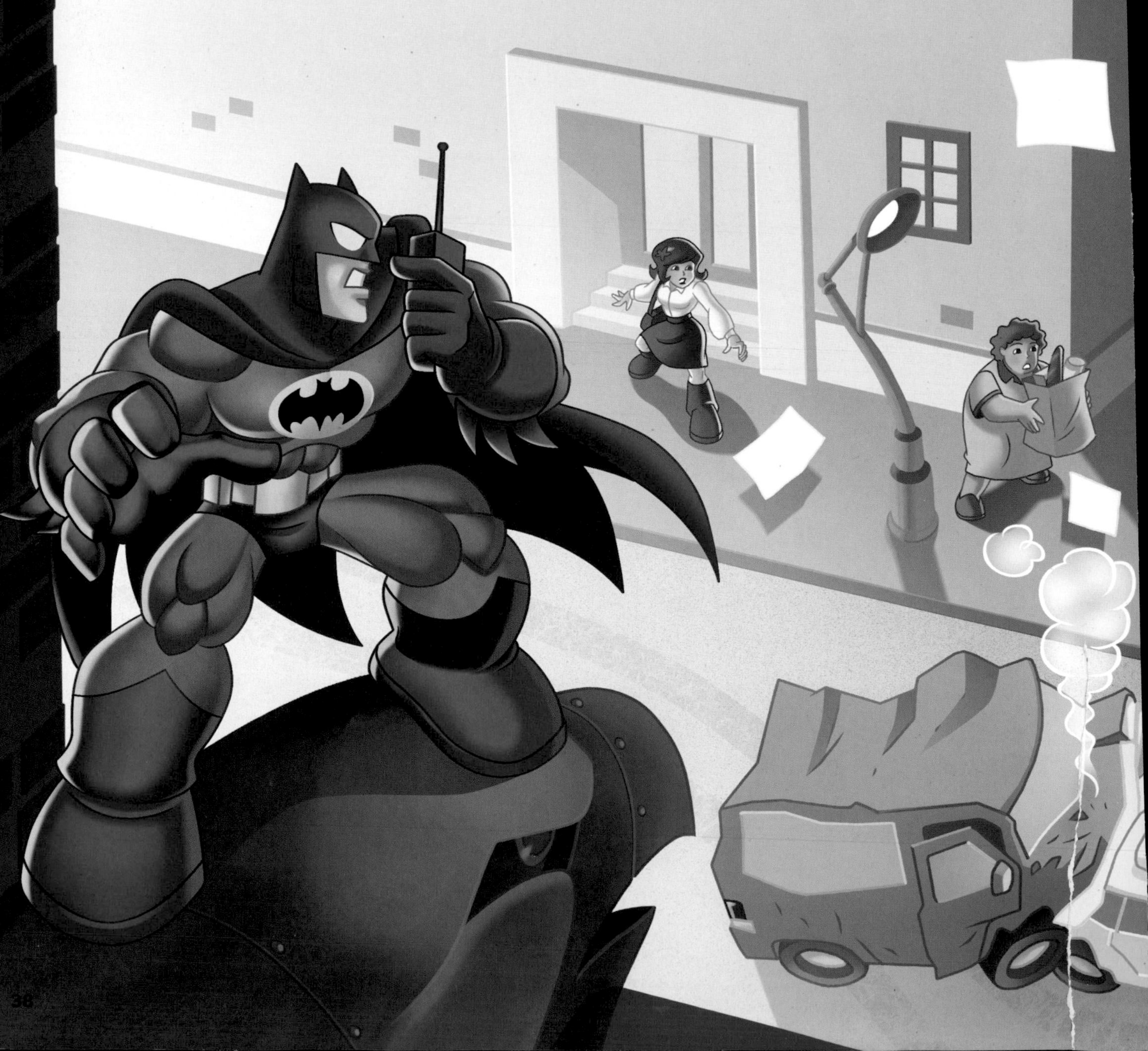

“We’re on our way!” the Super Friends responded.

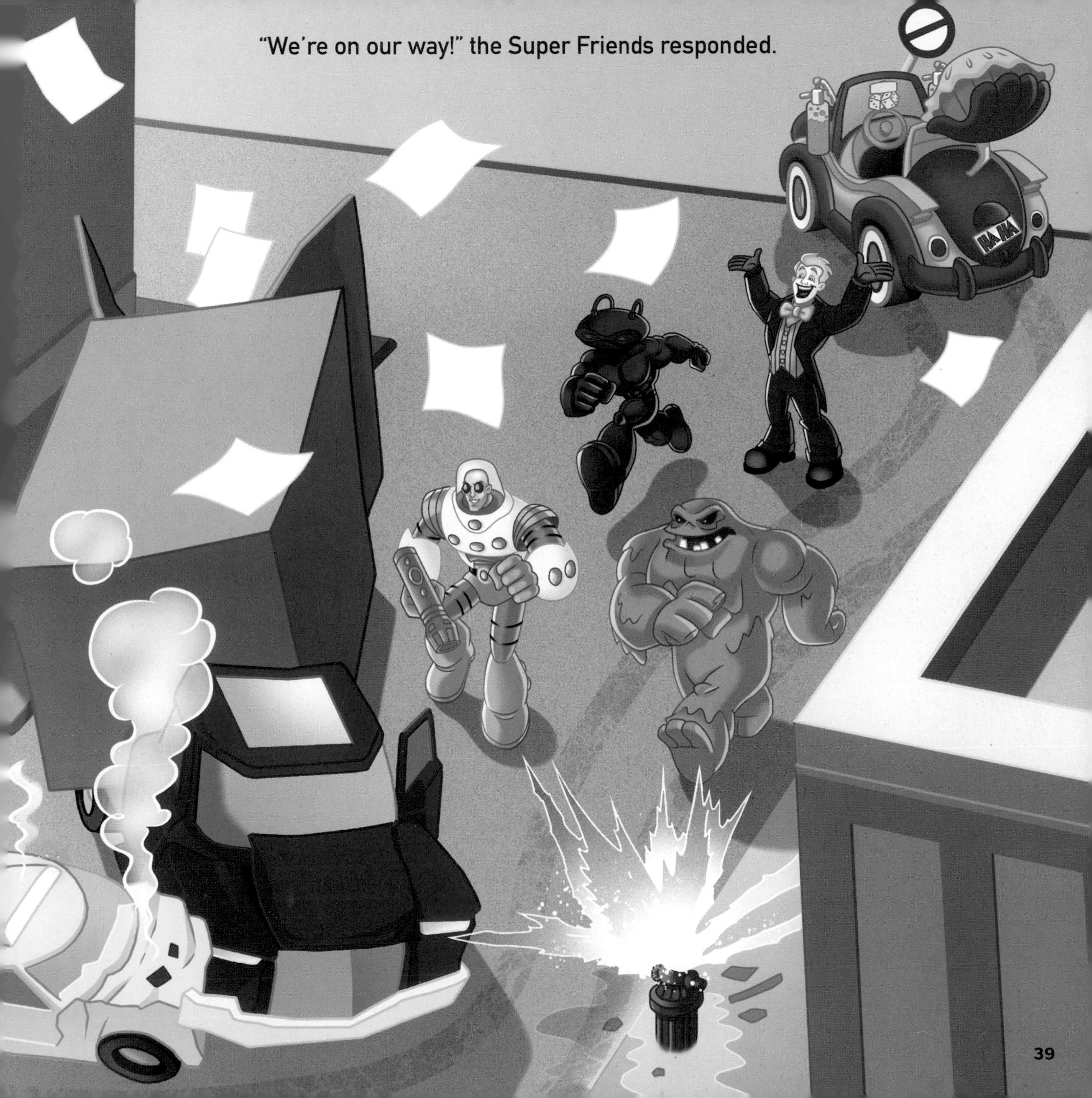
HA HA

Robin, Green Lantern, and Cyborg raced to the scene.

"The fun's over," Batman said to the bad guys. "It's time for you jailbirds to go back where you belong."

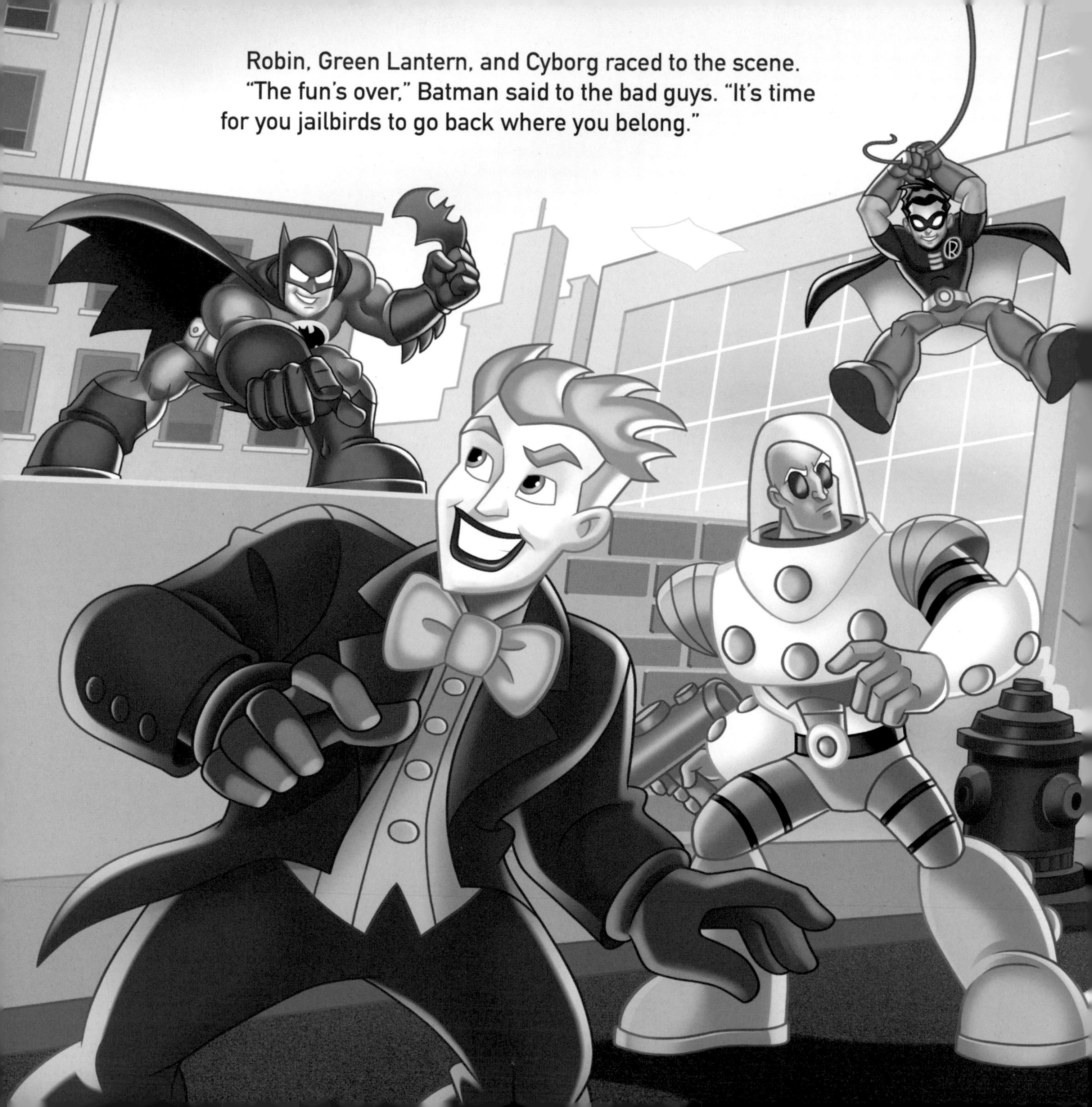

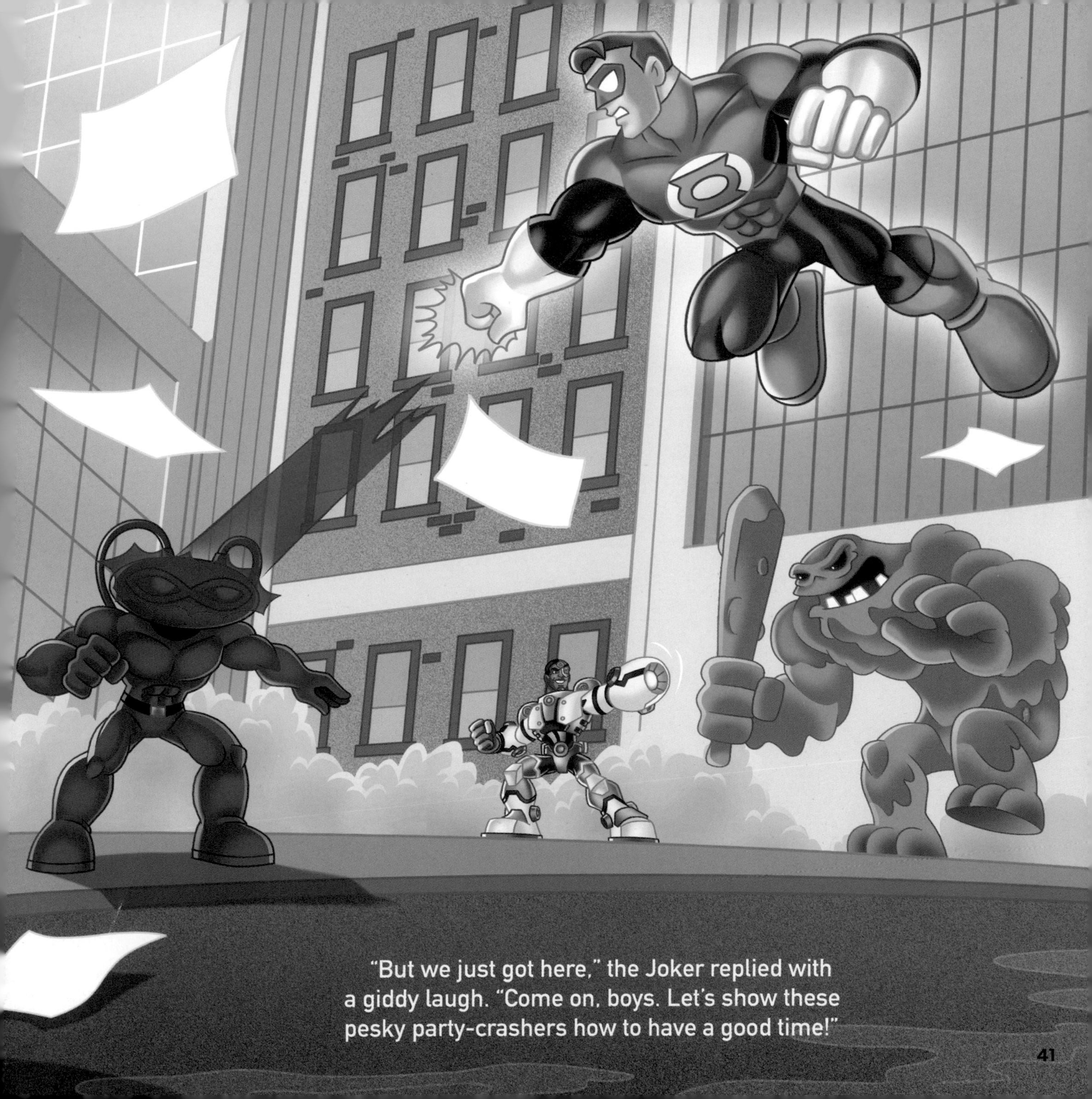

“But we just got here,” the Joker replied with a giddy laugh. “Come on, boys. Let’s show these pesky party-crashers how to have a good time!”

"I can take care of the Super Friends myself," Black Manta growled. He fired red laser blasts at Green Lantern. Thinking quickly, Green Lantern created a mirror with his energy ring to deflect the beams.

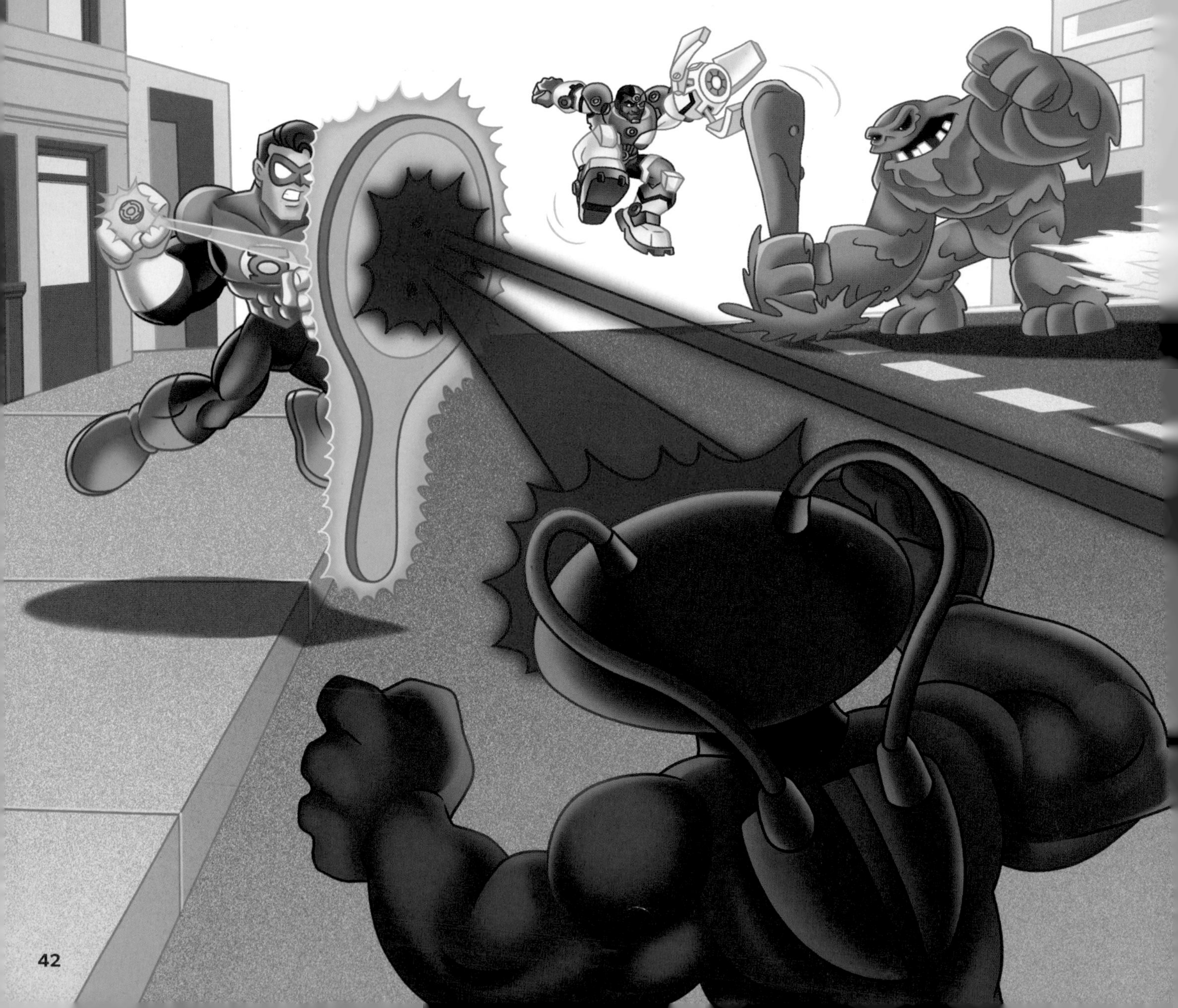

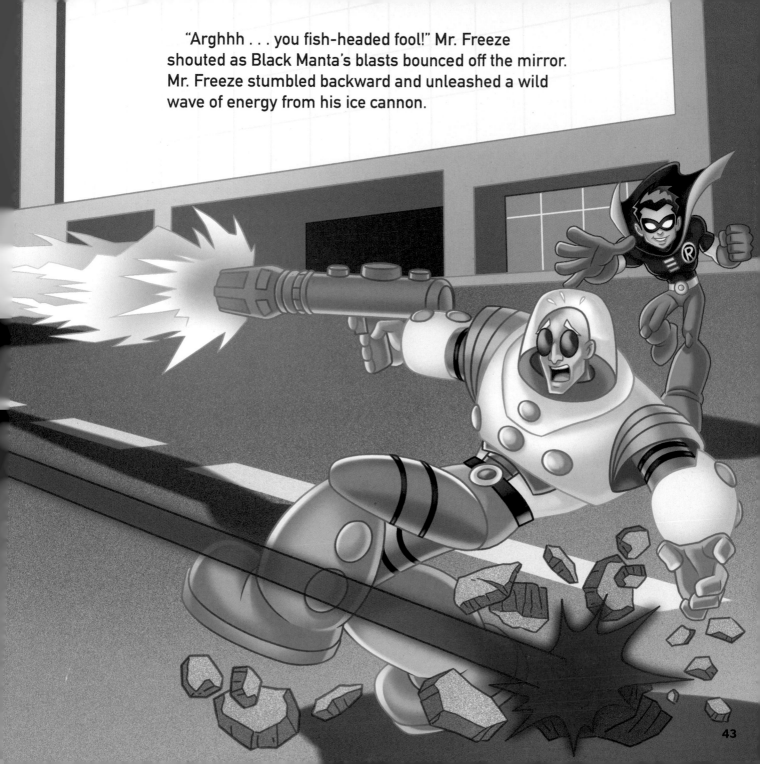

"Arghhh . . . you fish-headed fool!" Mr. Freeze shouted as Black Manta's blasts bounced off the mirror. Mr. Freeze stumbled backward and unleashed a wild wave of energy from his ice cannon.

Cyborg was busy trying to subdue Clayface, but the gooey bad guy kept slipping free from the machine man's mechanical fists.

"Here's mud in your eye," Clayface snarled, his arm turning into a huge clay club. But just as he was about to swing it, Mr. Freeze's energy wave froze him in solid ice!

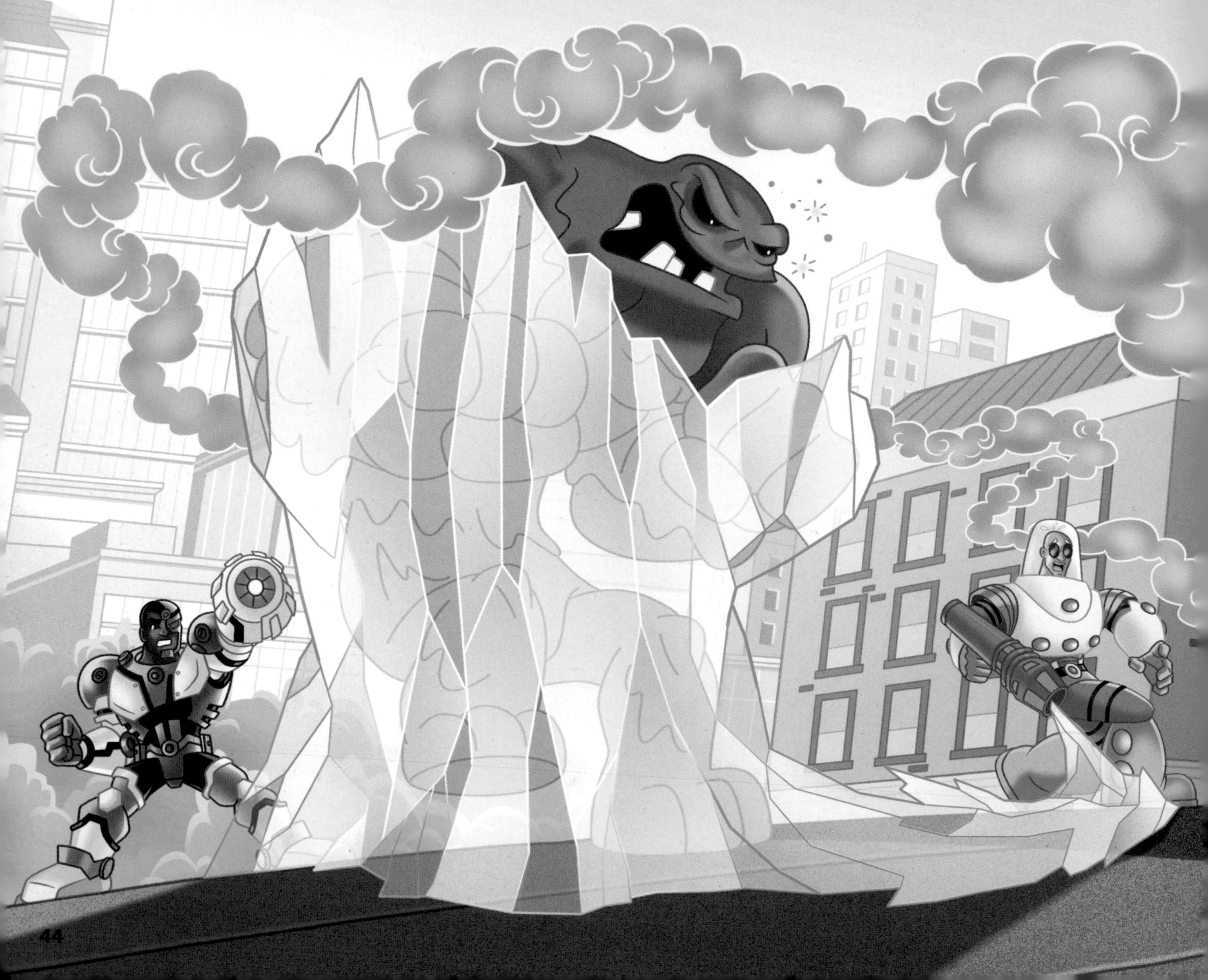

"You made mud-cicles!" the Joker cried gleefully. "*Now* it's a party. Let's all have a laugh!"

The Joker tossed a can of laughing gas at the Super Friends. Batman threw a Batarang, causing the gas to release on the villains!

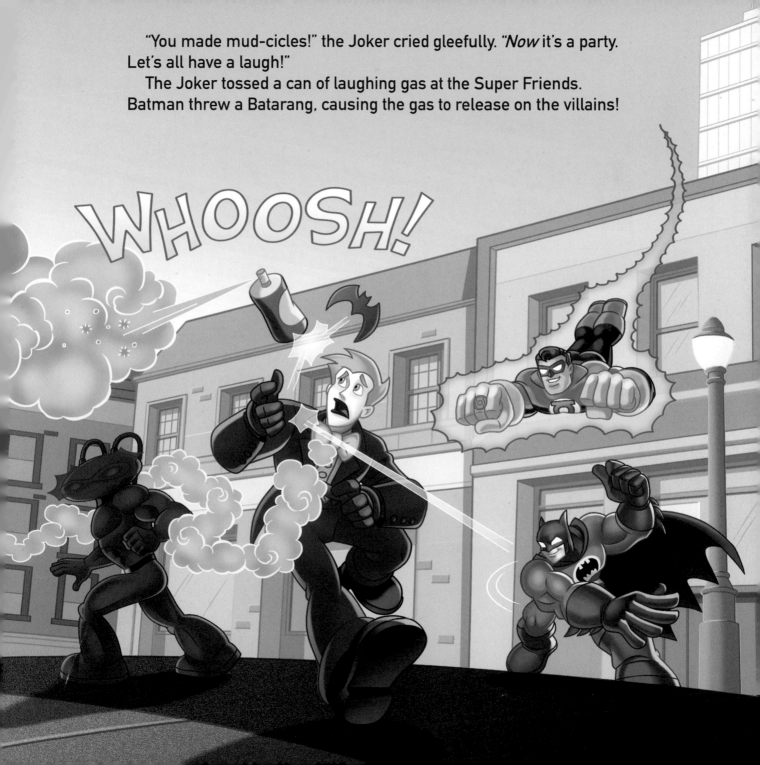

WHOOSH!

The green gas made the bad guys laugh so hard, they couldn't fight.

"Looks like teamwork has the last laugh," Batman said as the Super Friends easily rounded up the helpless villains.

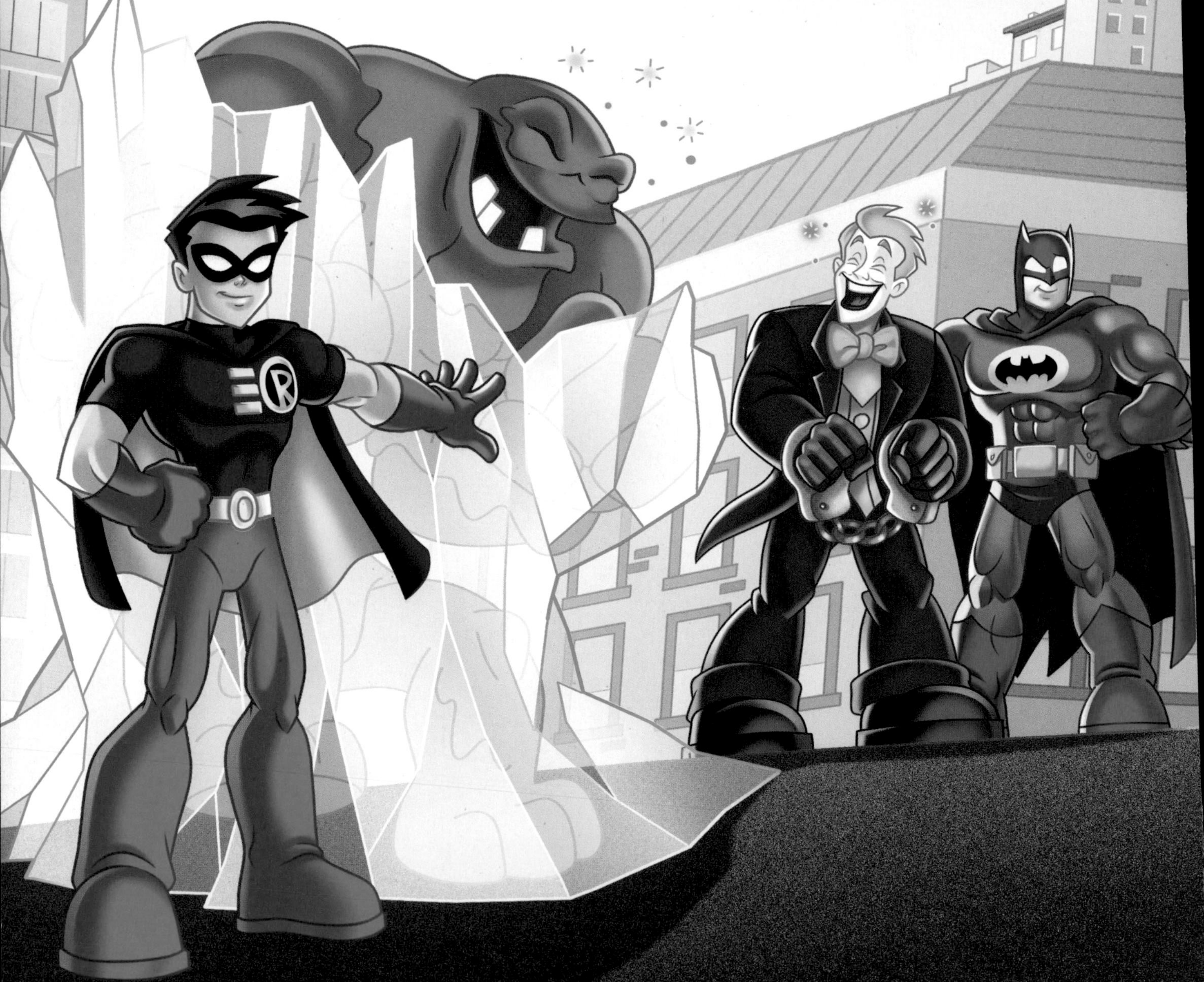

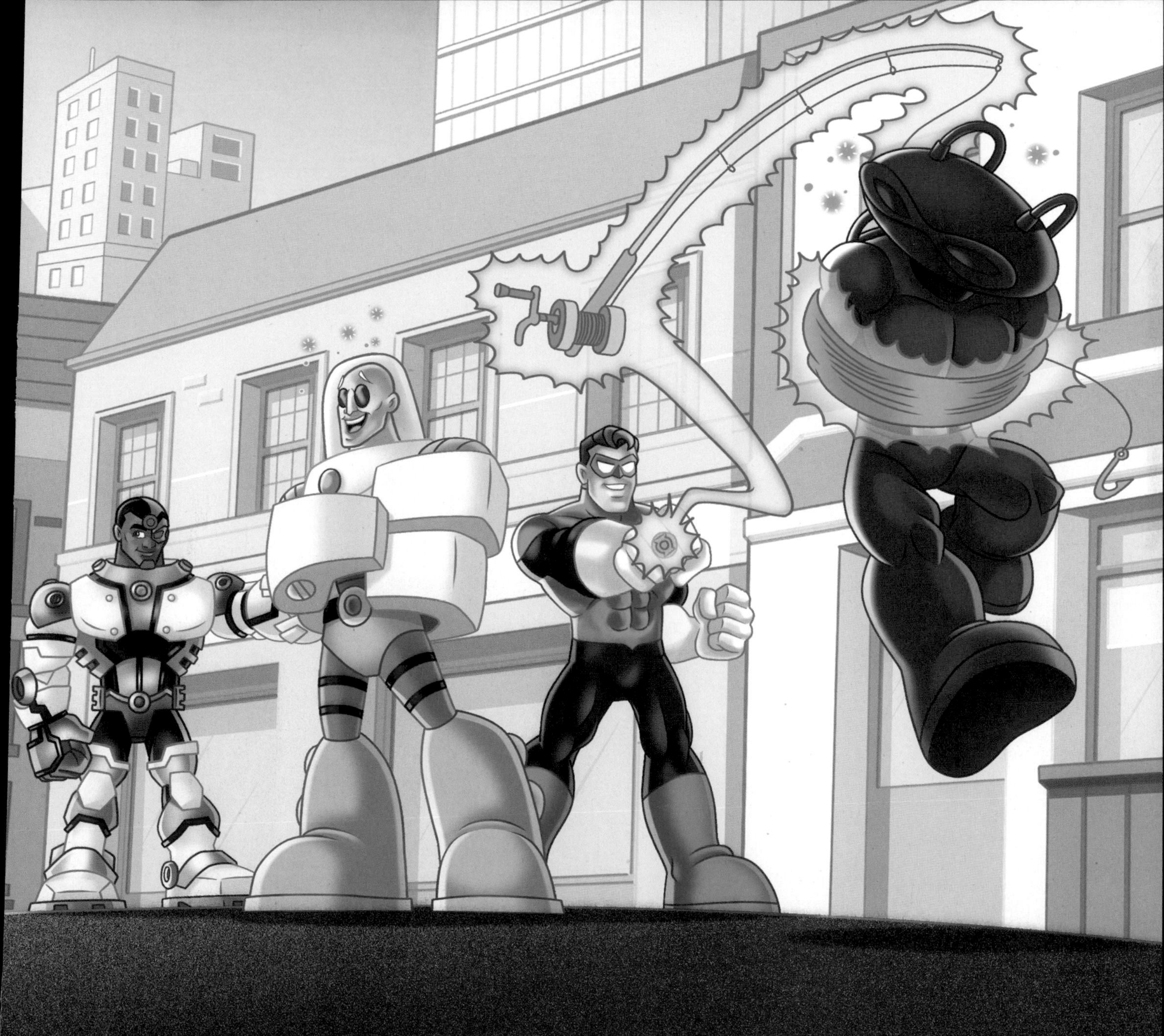

"Ha-ha. Very funny," the Joker managed to grumble between giggles. "But we'll be back before you know it!"

The Super Friends sent the bad guys back to jail, and all was quiet again for a while. But then—**KA-RUNCH!**

"Are you apes ready to help me with some monkey business?" Gorilla Grodd roared, pulling the prison doors off their hinges.

"Jailbreak!" the villains shouted. "Let's go!"

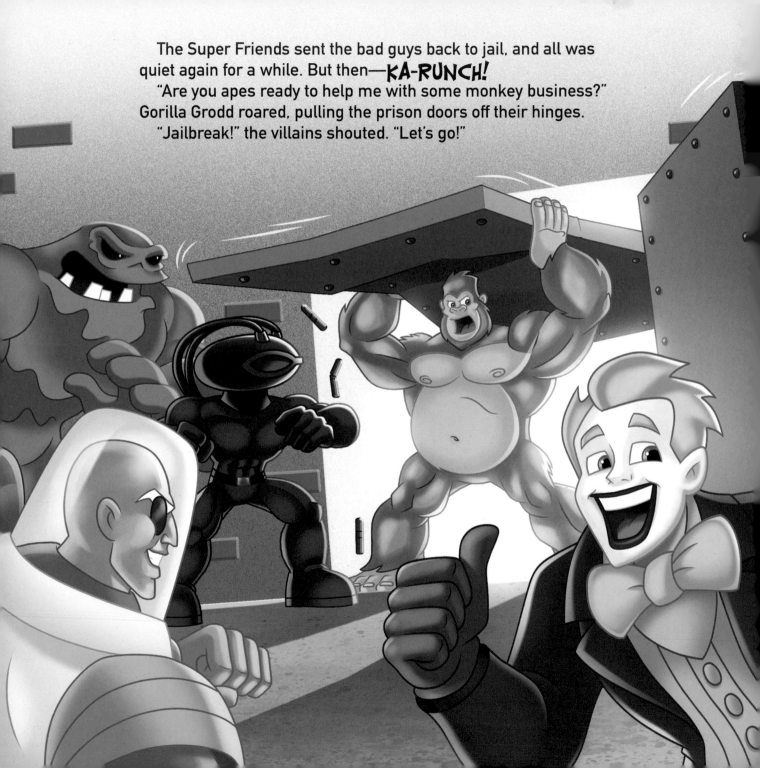

DC SUPER FRIENDS™

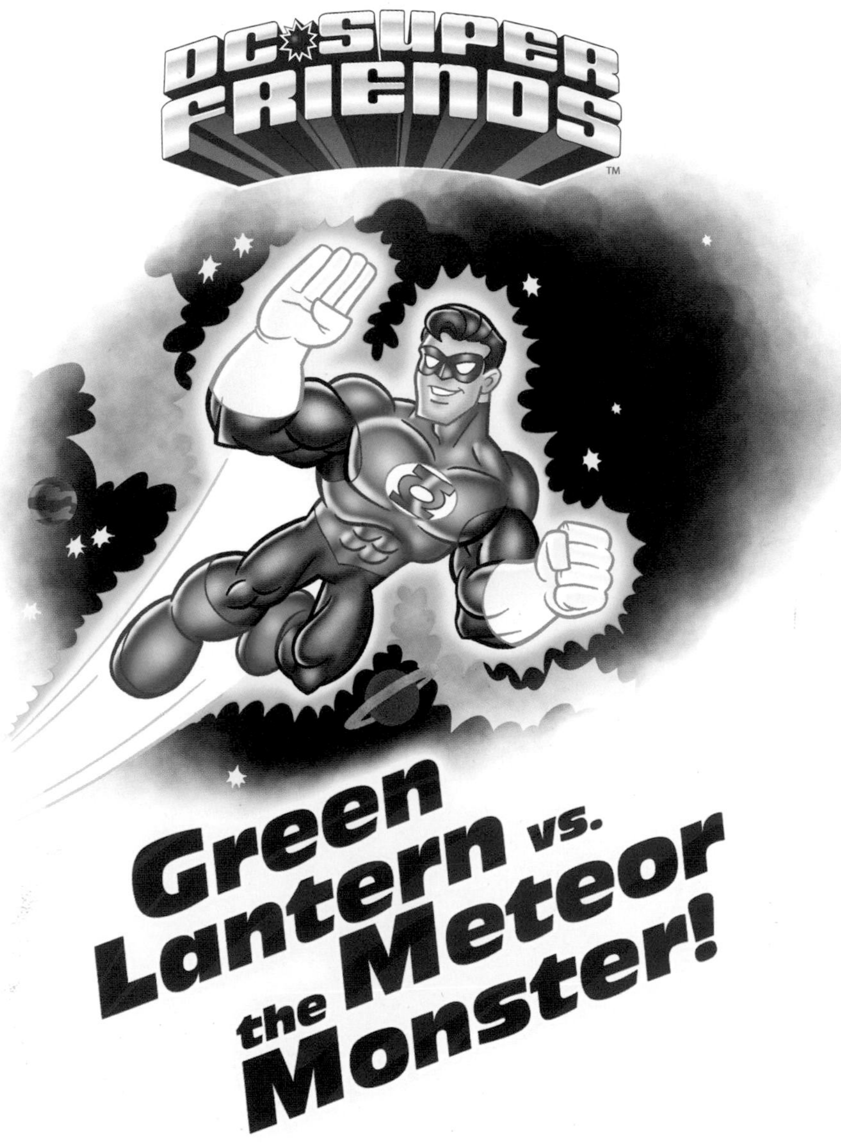

Green Lantern vs. the Meteor Monster!

By D. R. Shealy

Illustrated by Erik Doescher, Mike DeCarlo, and David Tanguay

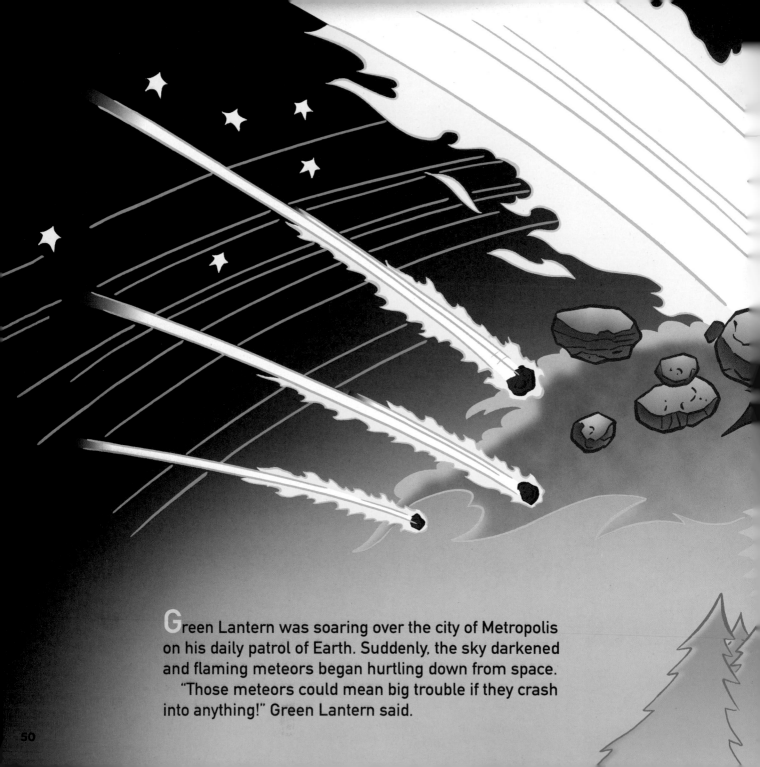

Green Lantern was soaring over the city of Metropolis on his daily patrol of Earth. Suddenly, the sky darkened and flaming meteors began hurtling down from space.

"Those meteors could mean big trouble if they crash into anything!" Green Lantern said.

He smashed the closest meteor into a million tiny pieces by creating a shield with his amazing power ring.

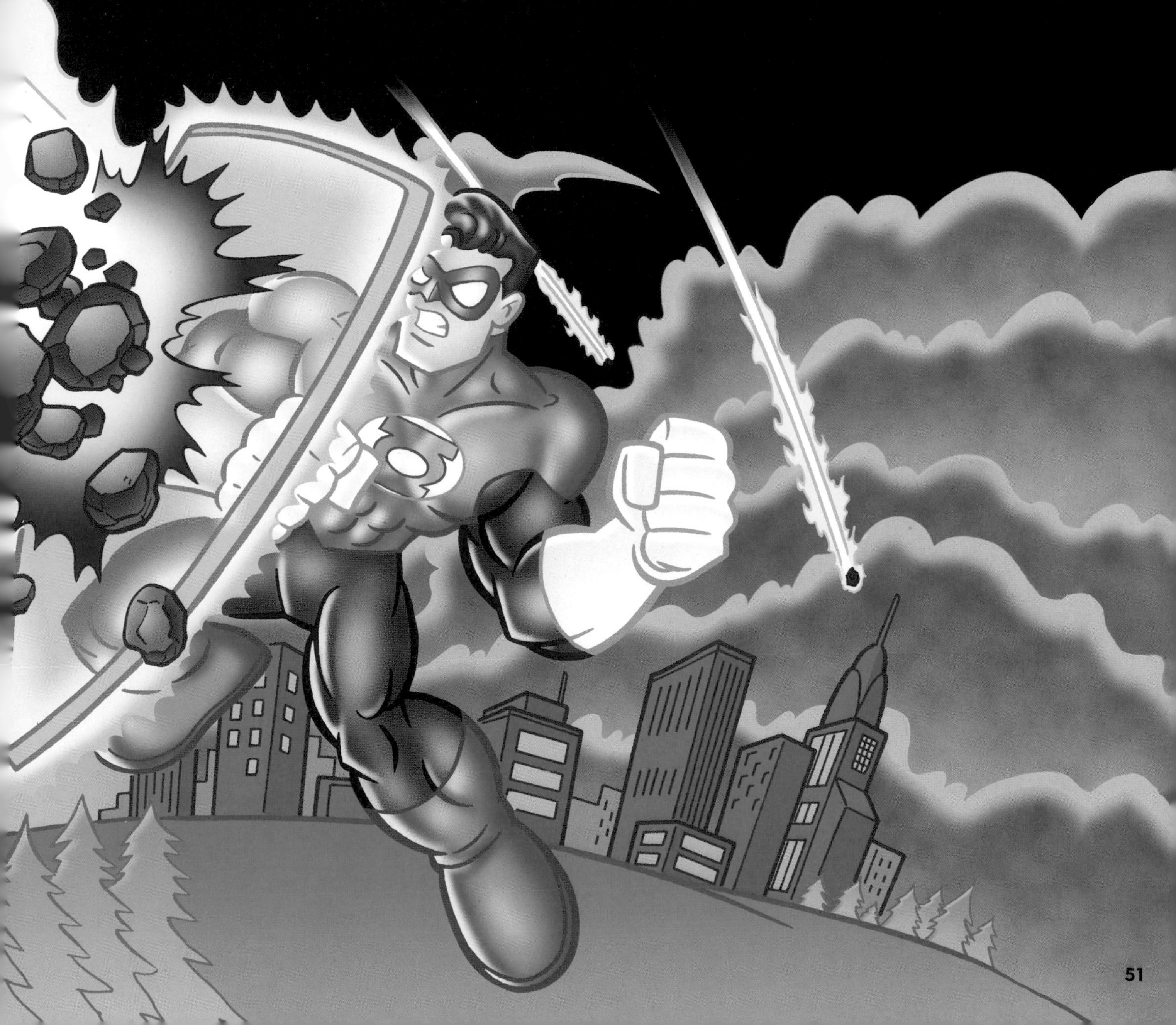

Green Lantern quickly created a large net with his ring. He flew through the sky, scooping up the meteors before they struck the city. But one fiery meteor escaped his net!

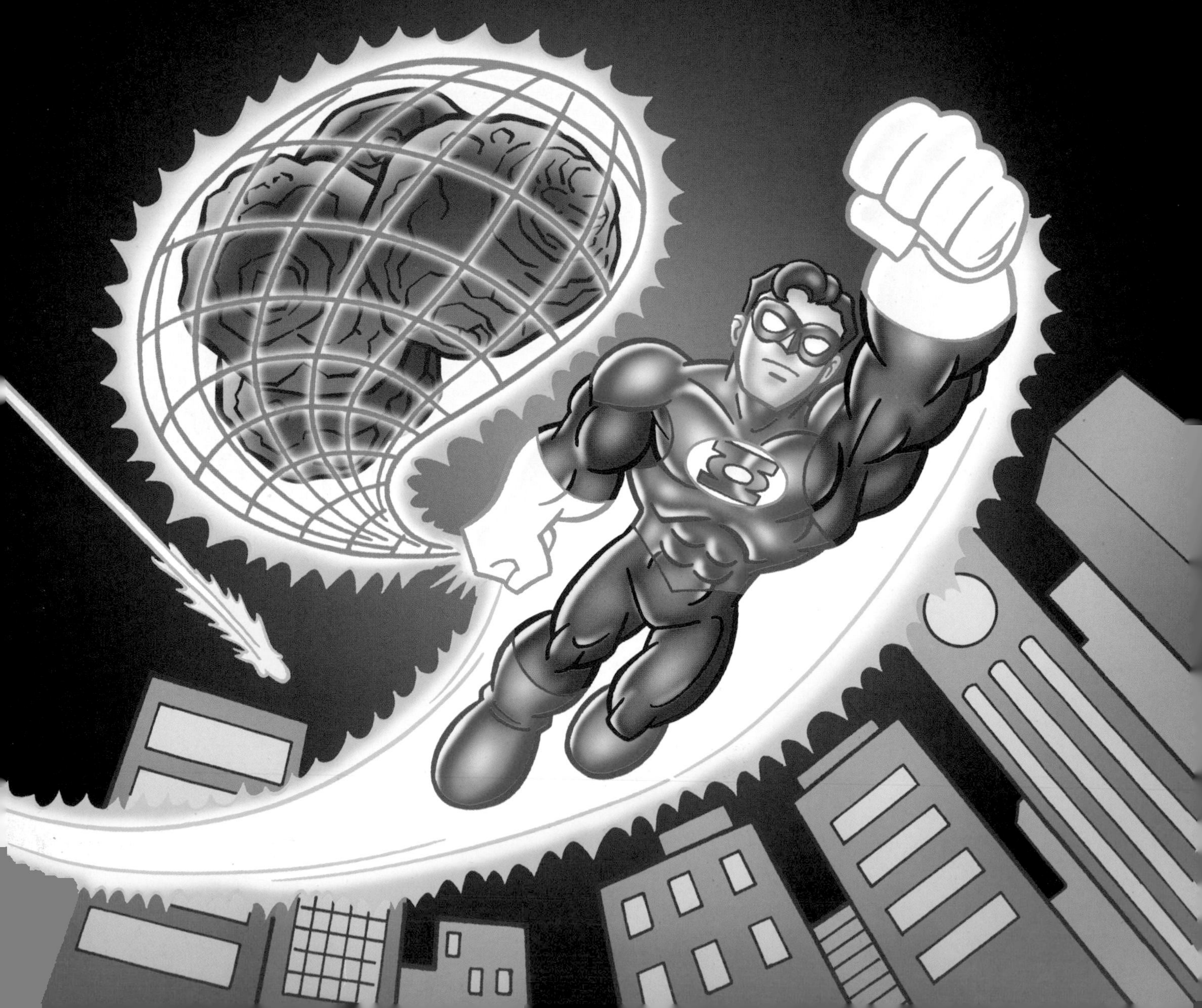

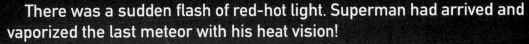

There was a sudden flash of red-hot light. Superman had arrived and vaporized the last meteor with his heat vision!

"Good work!" Green Lantern shouted.

"Let's get going," Superman replied. "Batman and Hawkman need us."

Green Lantern and Superman quickly met up with Hawkman and Batman.

"My radar shows a giant meteor heading straight for Metropolis," Batman said over the Batwing's comlink.

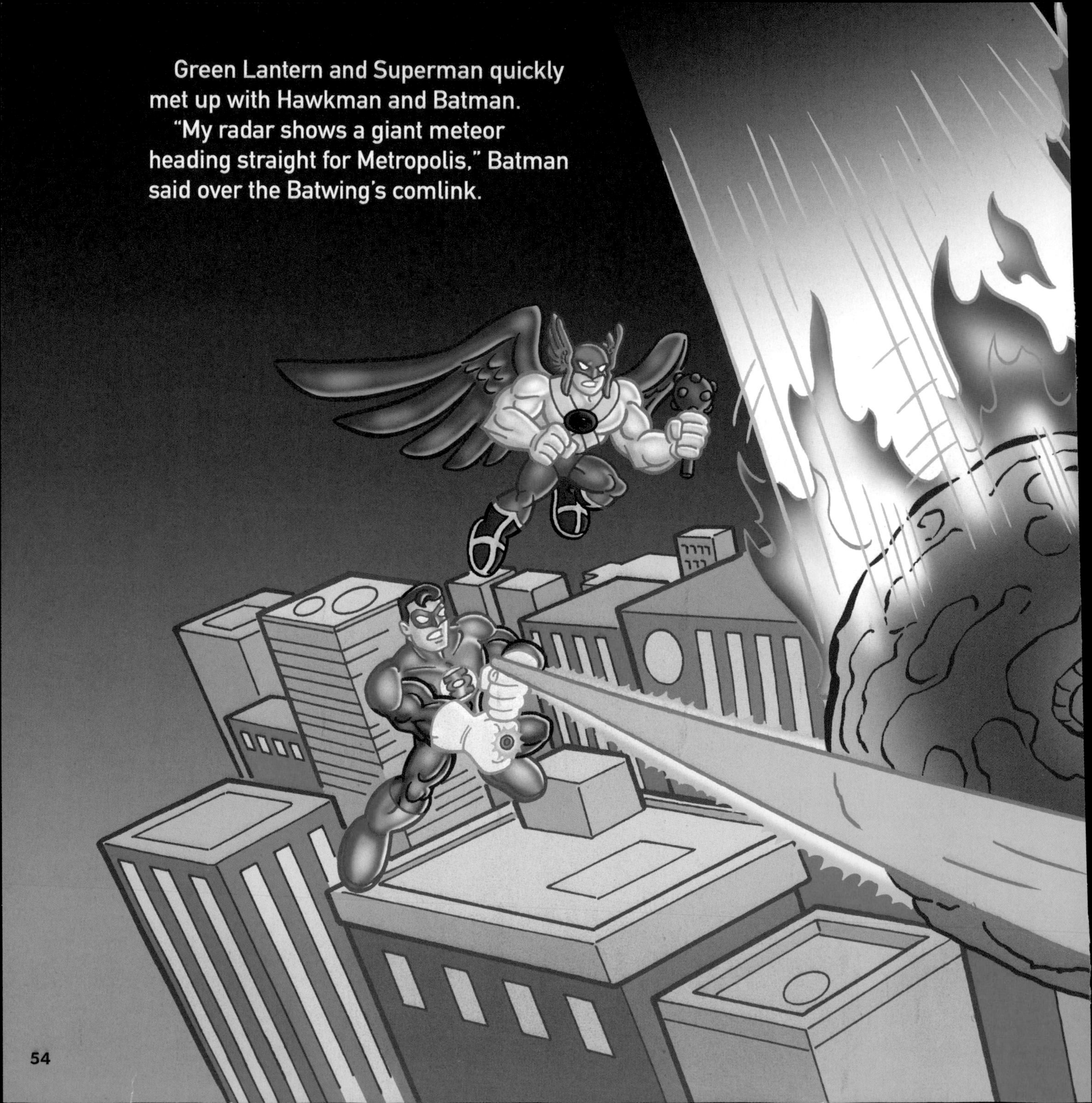

Green Lantern produced a long rubber band with his power ring. Superman grabbed one end, and the two heroes held on with every ounce of their strength as the meteor slammed into it and stretched it tight. SNAP! The meteor shot up and away from the city.

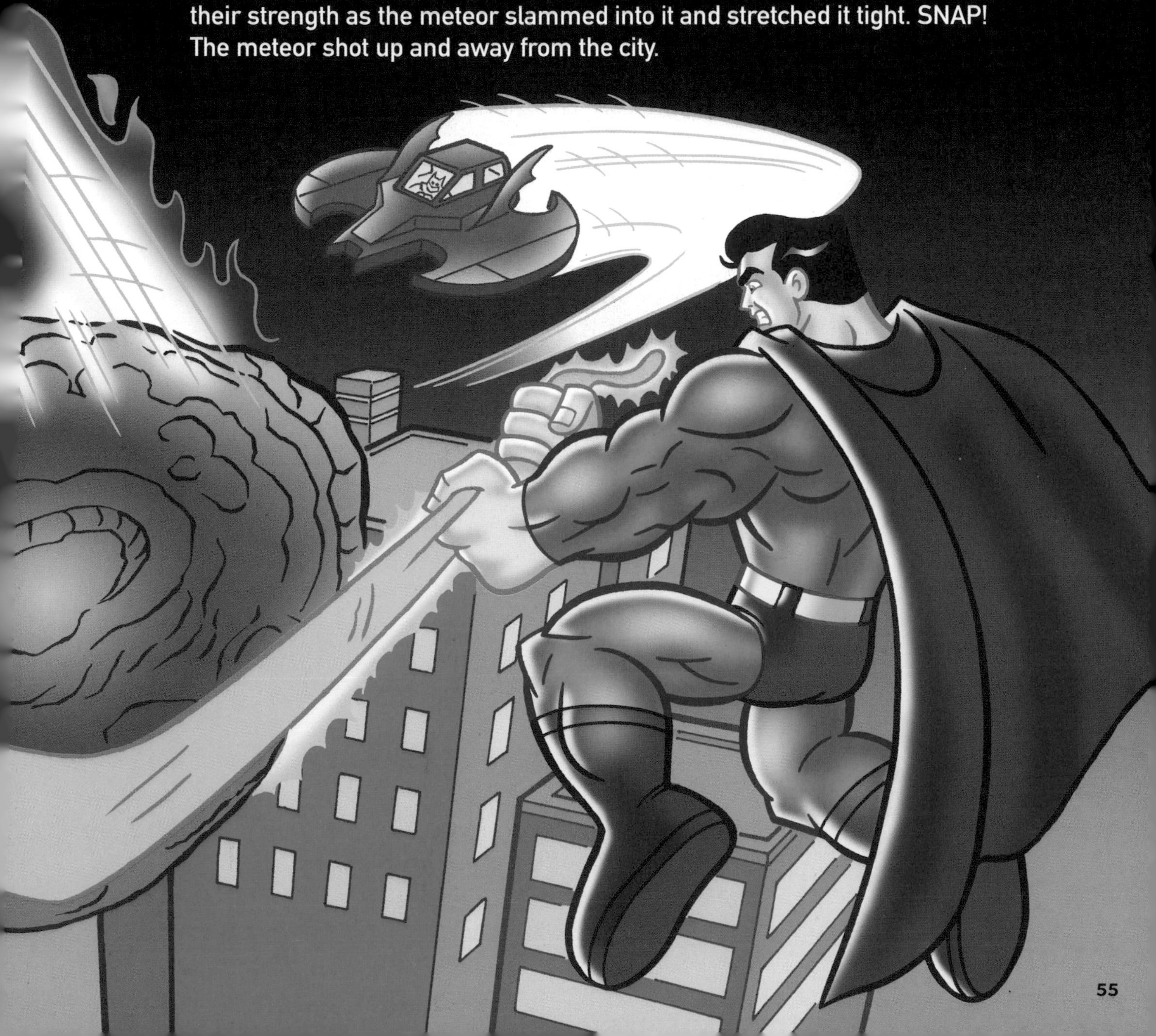

The Super Friends dashed to the impact site, where the meteor had landed. They peered into the smoldering crater.

"That meteorite doesn't look like the others," Green Lantern said, generating a force field to protect his friends from the hot space rock.

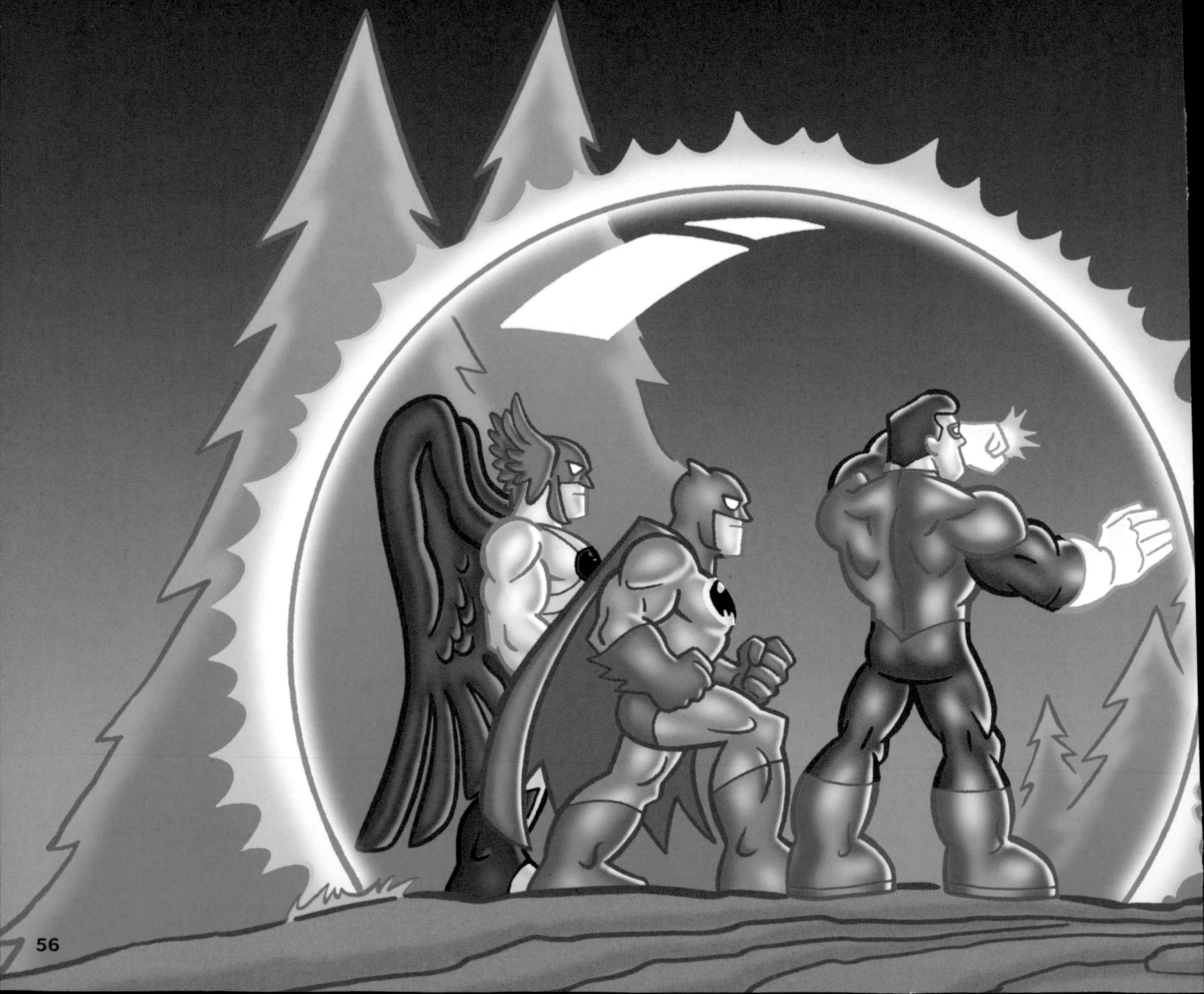

Superman scanned the meteorite with his X-ray vision and replied, "That's because it's a—"

"Look out!" Green Lantern shouted.

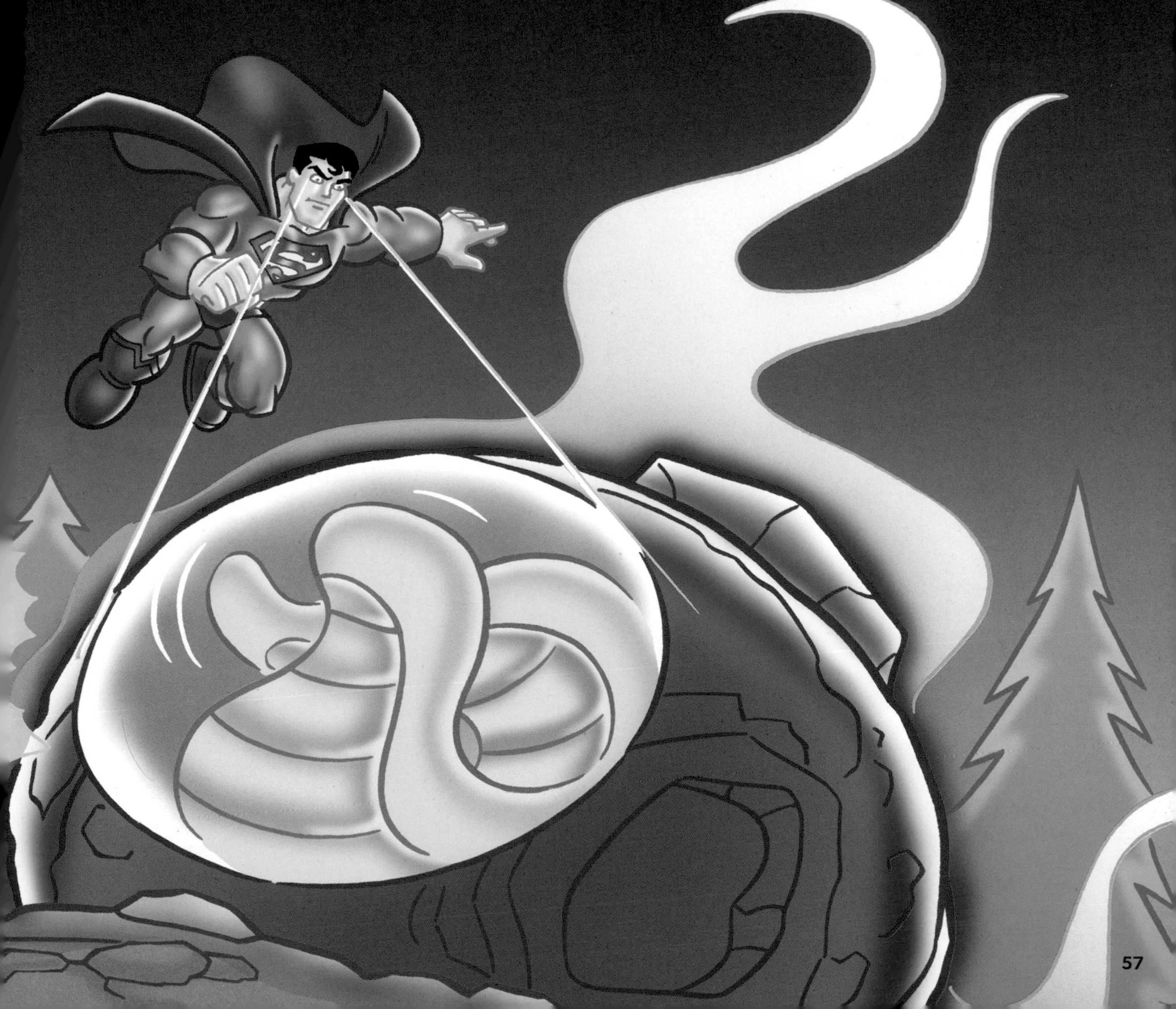

A giant alien burst out of the crumbling meteorite! "MMMMAAAAARRRAWWW!" it roared at the Super Friends.

"My power ring can translate alien languages," Green Lantern said. "Maybe I can talk to this creature."

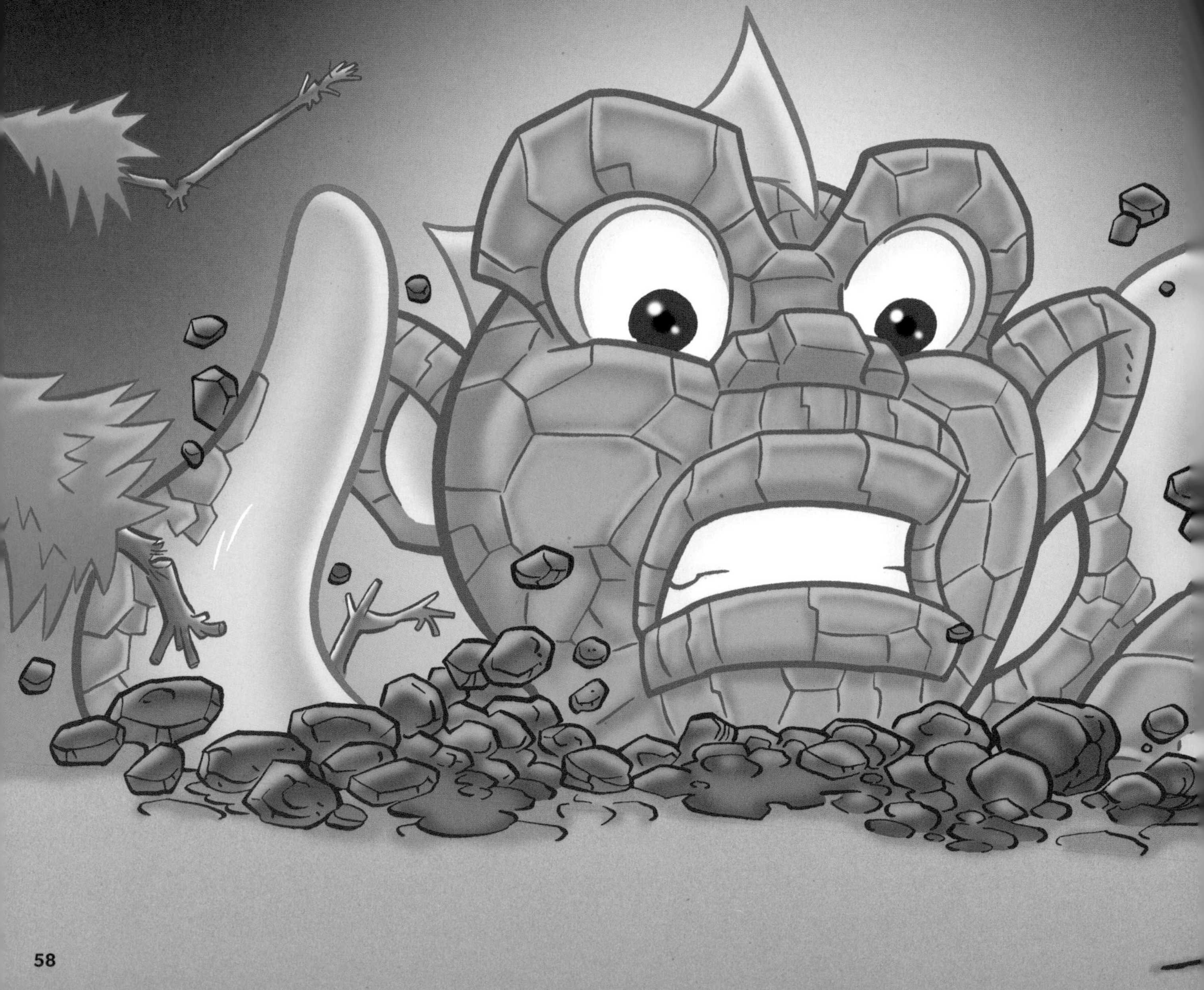

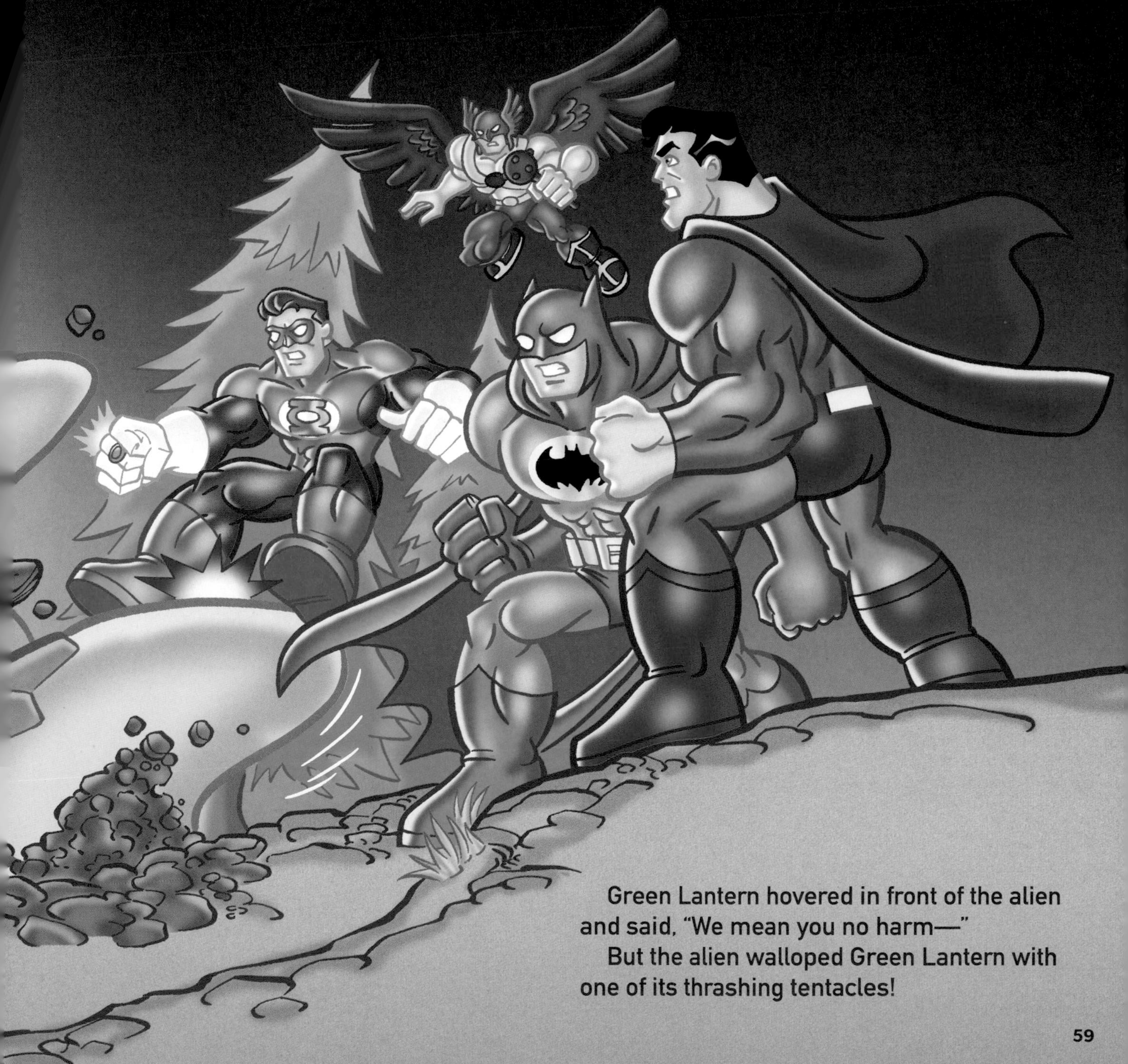

Green Lantern hovered in front of the alien and said, "We mean you no harm—"

But the alien walloped Green Lantern with one of its thrashing tentacles!

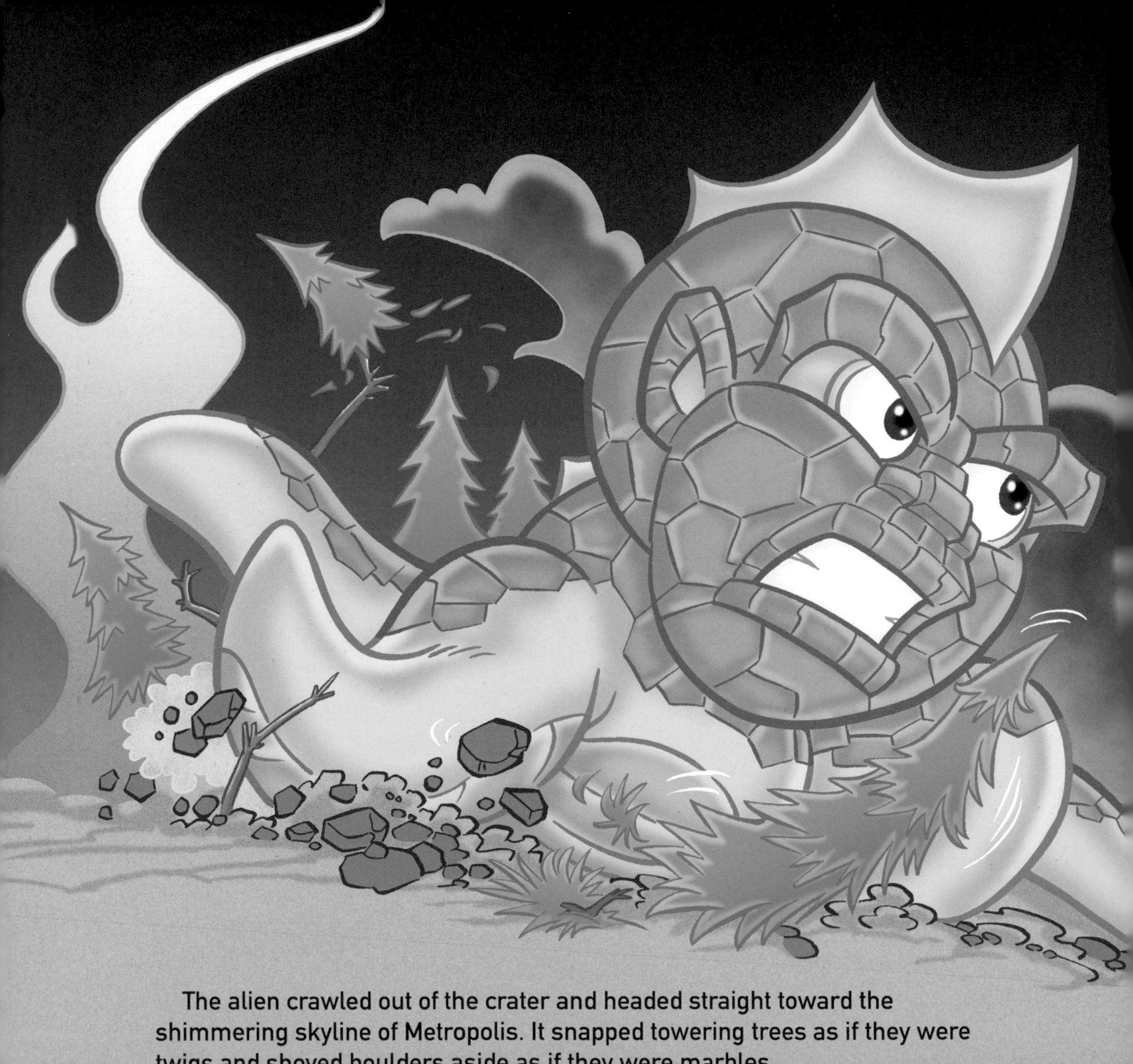

The alien crawled out of the crater and headed straight toward the shimmering skyline of Metropolis. It snapped towering trees as if they were twigs and shoved boulders aside as if they were marbles.

"We can't let it reach the city," Batman said. "That meteor monster will destroy everything in its path!"

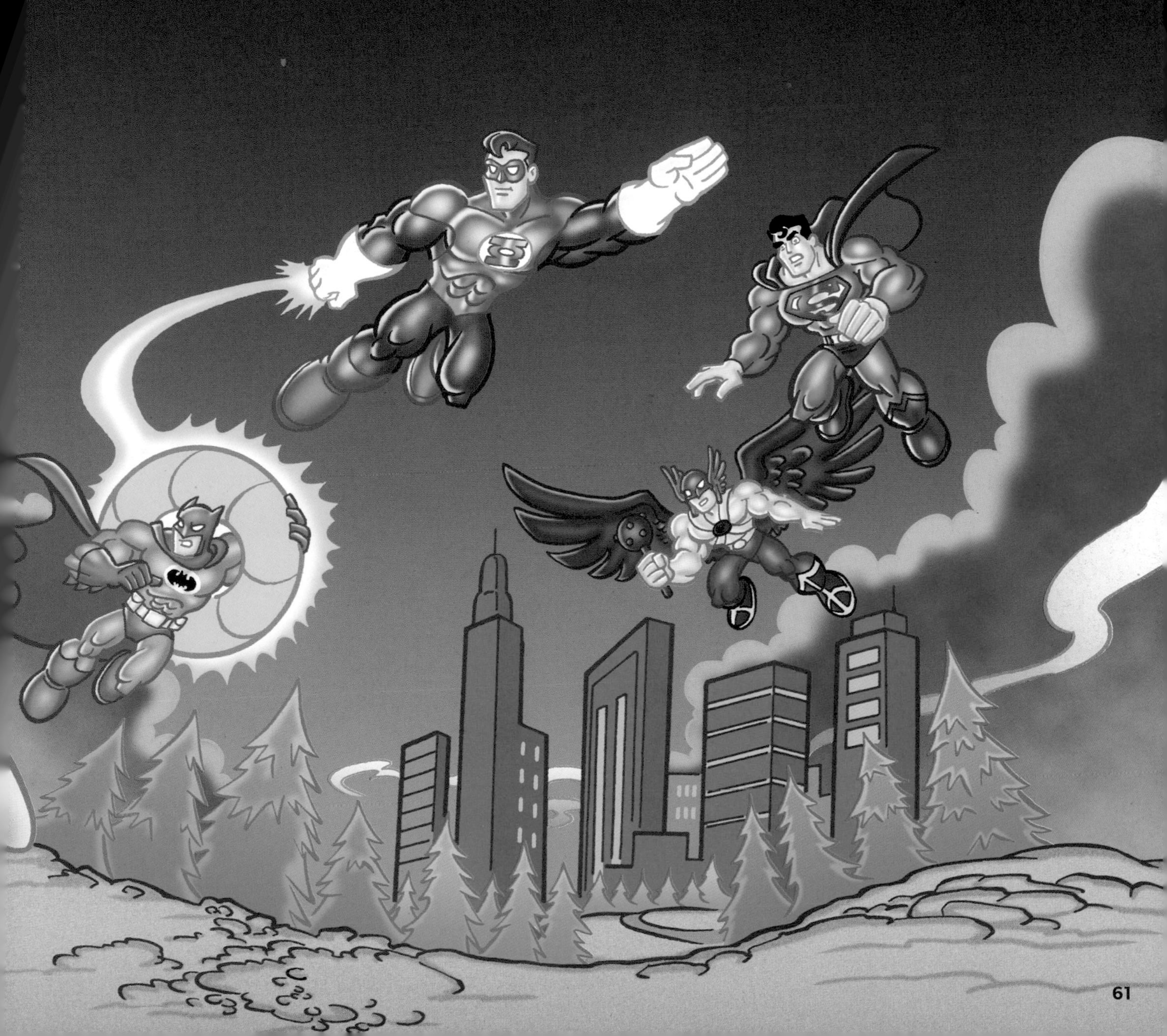

The Super Friends used all their powers, but the alien could not be stopped. Its skin was harder than rock. Batman's Batarangs bounced off it. Hawkman's mace couldn't dent it. And Superman's heat vision only made the alien angrier!

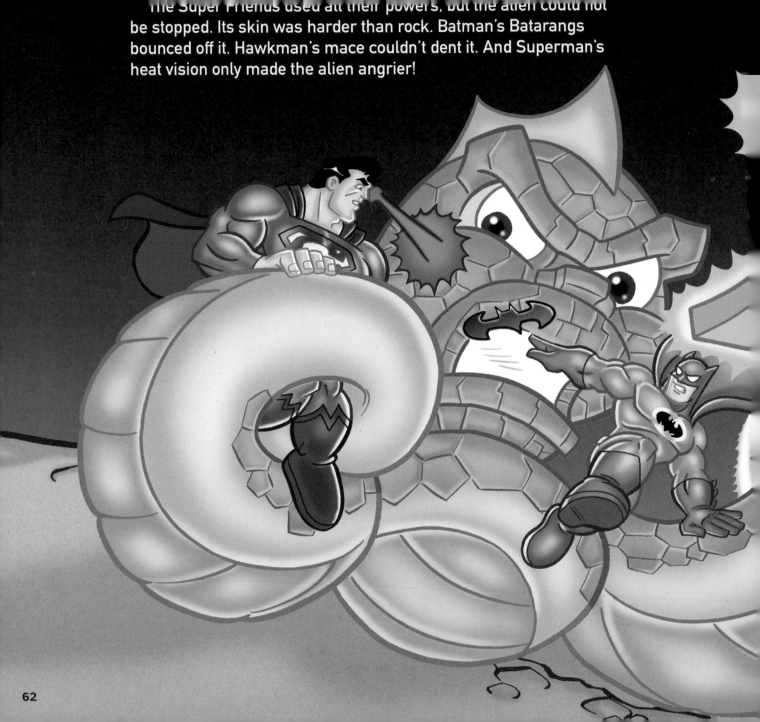

Green Lantern created a giant green bulldozer blade and pushed against the alien with all his might.

"We're not even slowing it down," Green Lantern said.

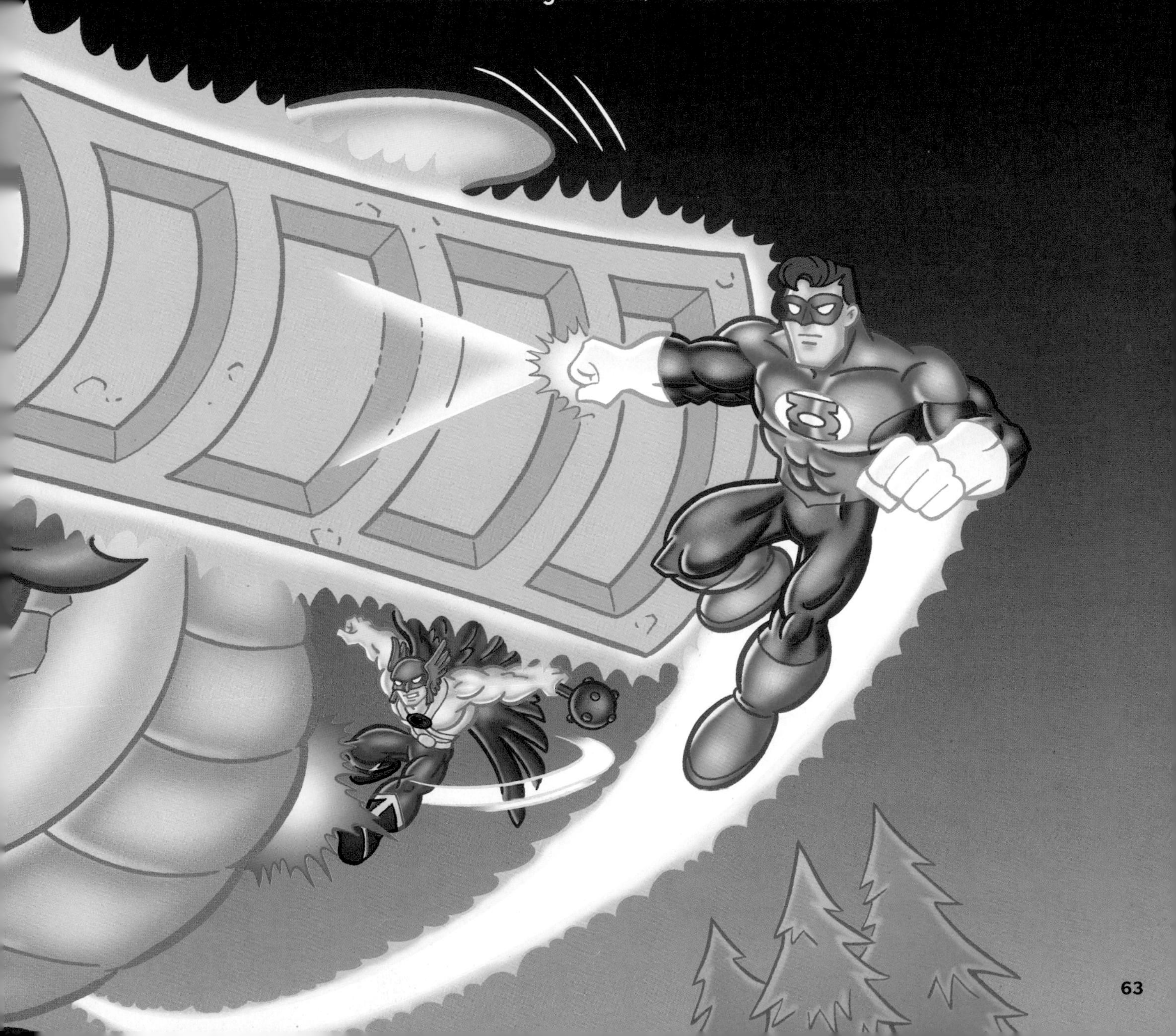

Suddenly, a dark shadow passed over the Super Friends. They looked up to see two much larger aliens descending from the sky!

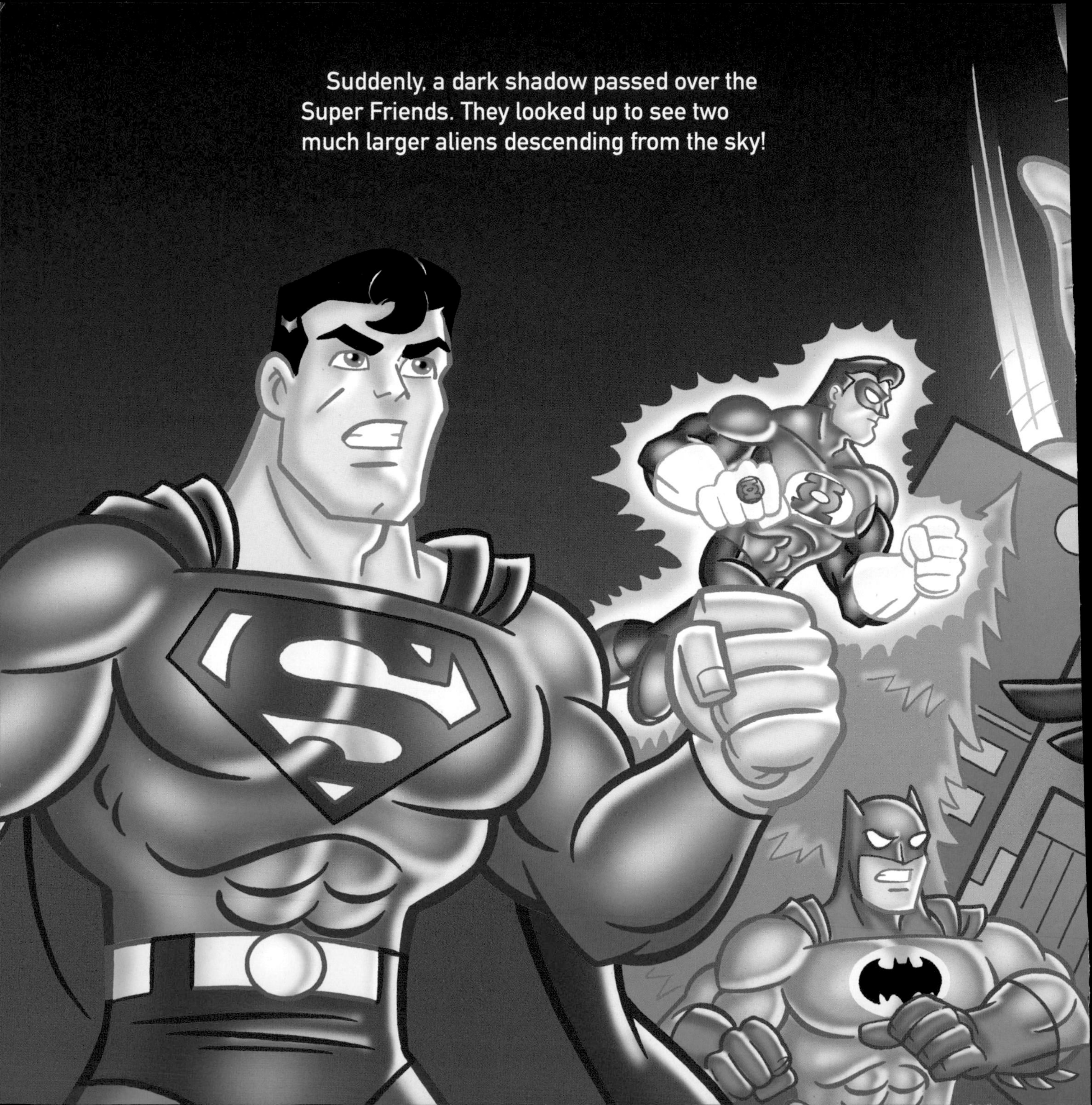

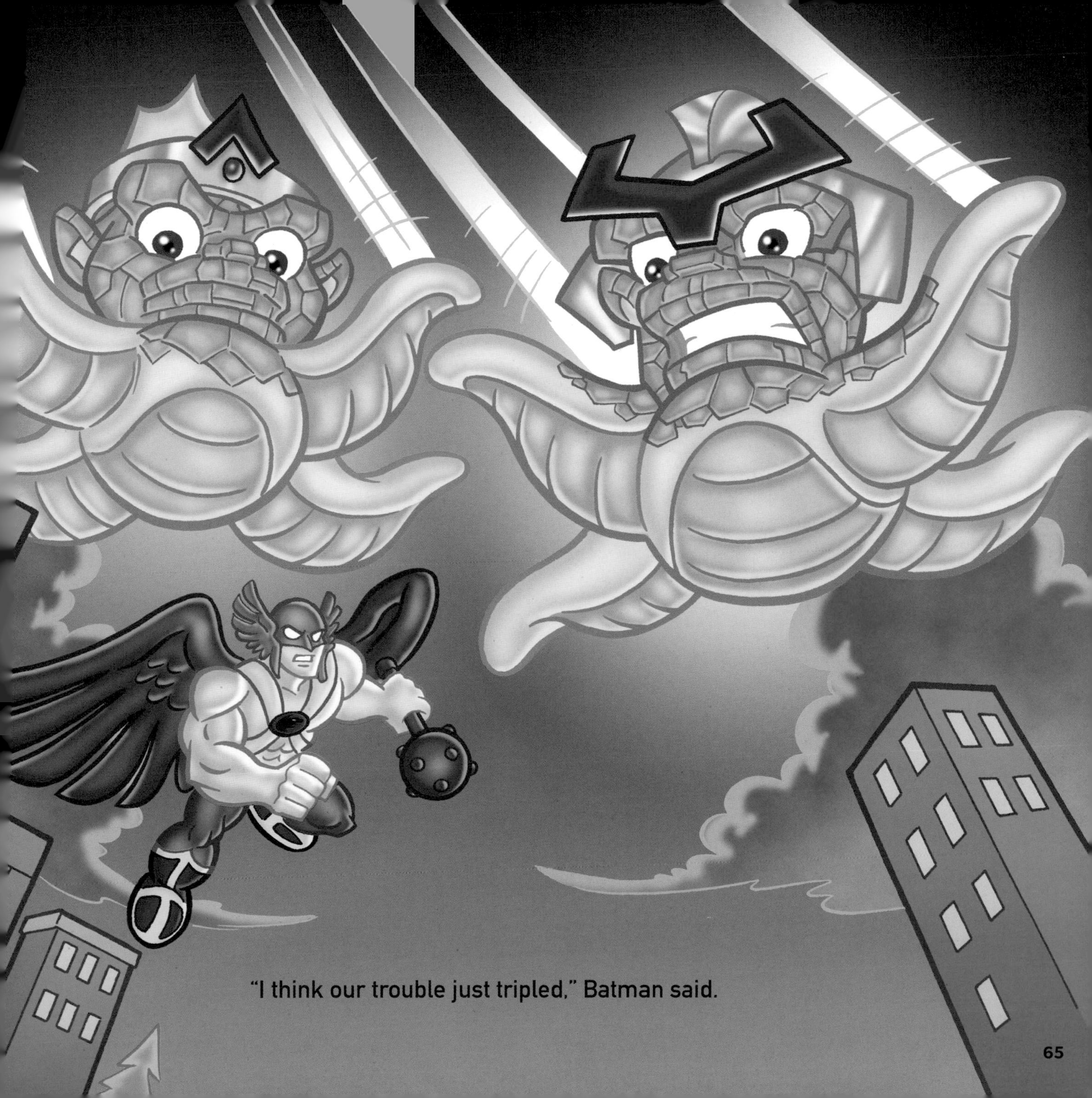

“I think our trouble just tripled,” Batman said.

"MMMAAAAARRRAWWW!" the small alien howled.

"I've got it!" Green Lantern shouted. "Follow me—I'm going to need everyone's help."

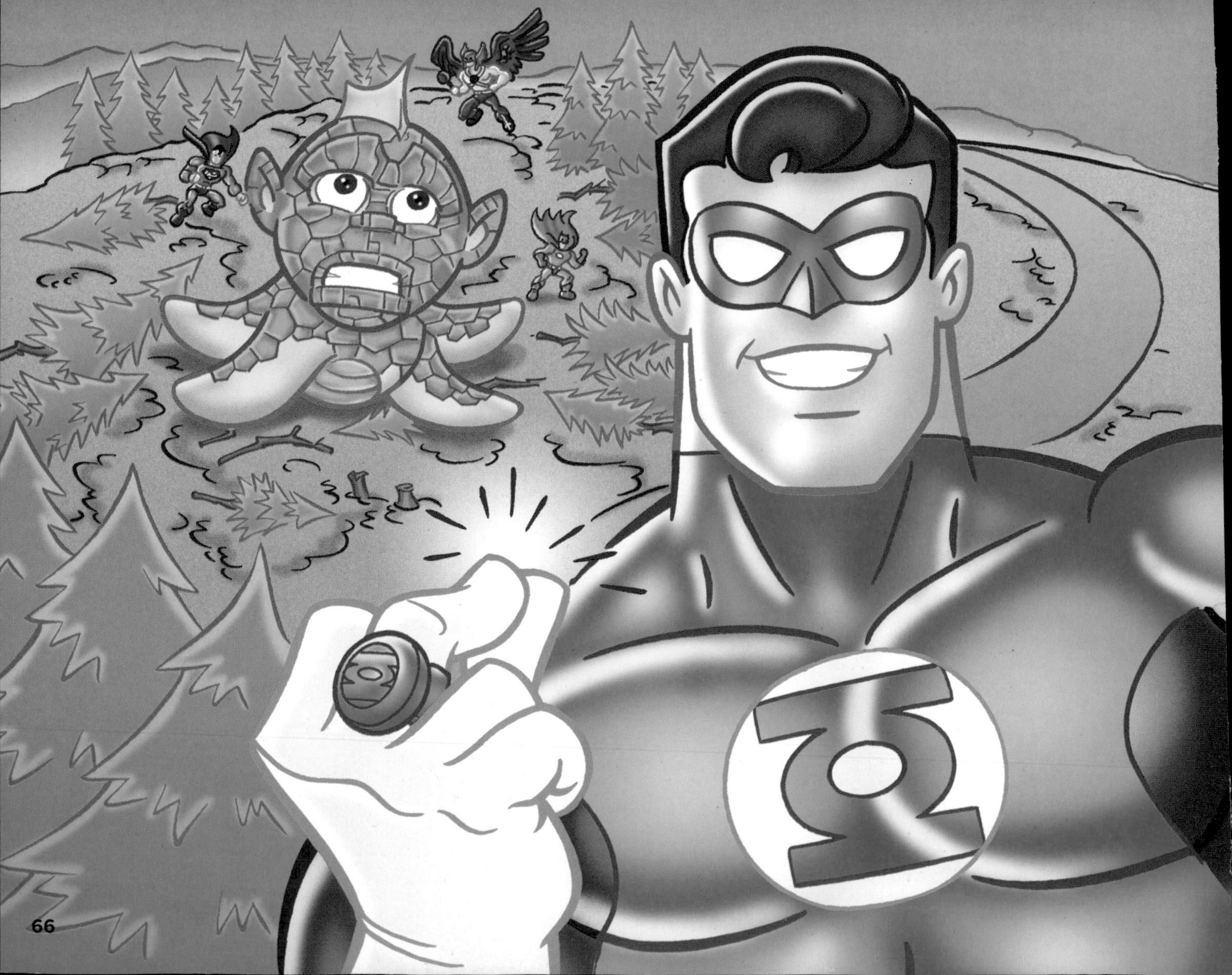

Green Lantern used his power ring to slip a giant fireman's trampoline under the alien. Superman and Hawkman gripped the frame.

"Now lift . . . ," Green Lantern called out, "gently!"

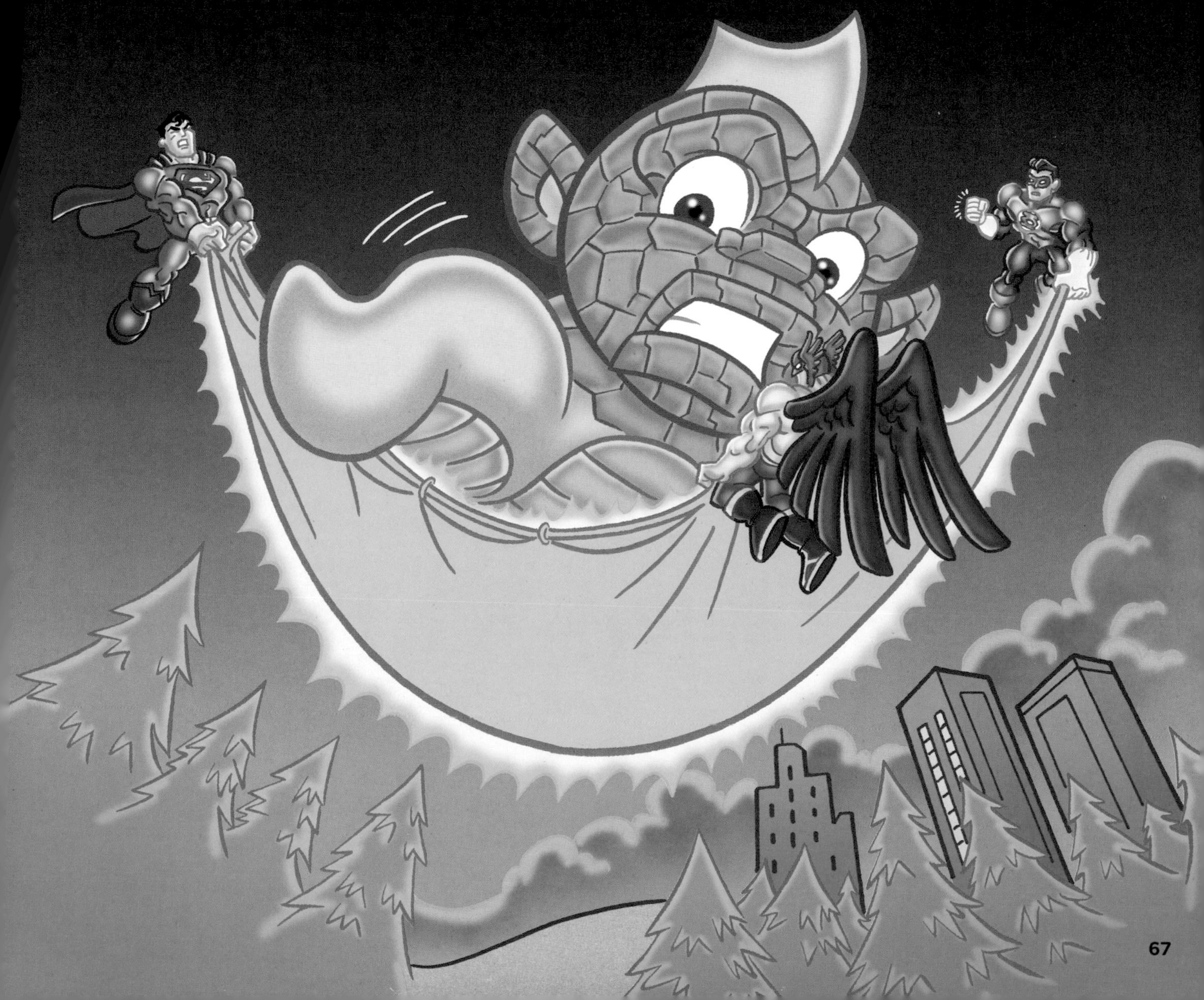

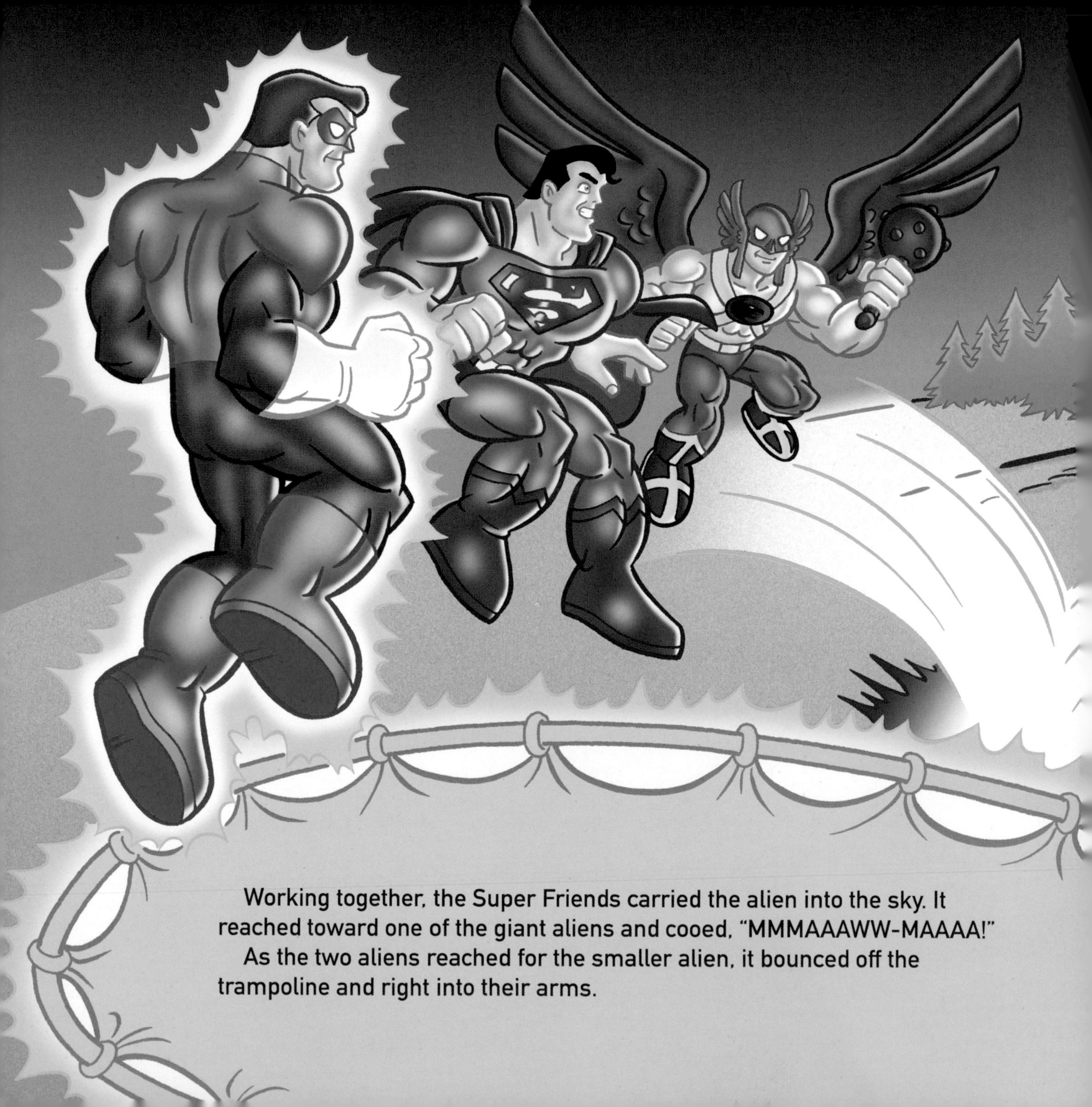

Working together, the Super Friends carried the alien into the sky. It reached toward one of the giant aliens and cooed, "MMMAAAWW-MAAAA!"

As the two aliens reached for the smaller alien, it bounced off the trampoline and right into their arms.

"We didn't mean any harm to your baby," Green Lantern explained through his power ring translator. "It's just that he's a *very* big, um . . . boy."

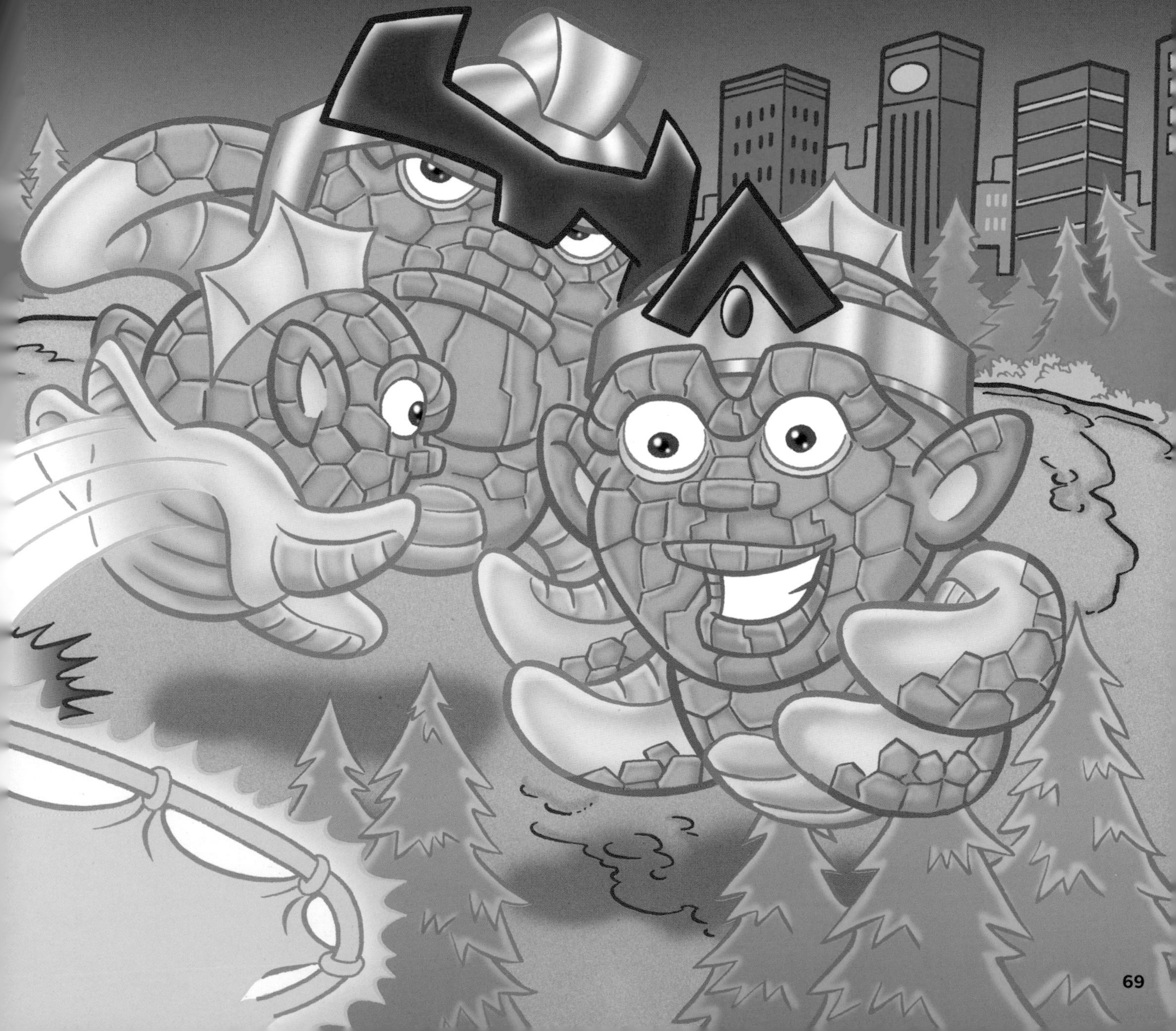

Green Lantern led the alien family back into space.

"You were on your way to the Omega Centauri galaxy? That meteor storm really *did* throw you off course!" Green Lantern said to the aliens. "Let me show you the way home."

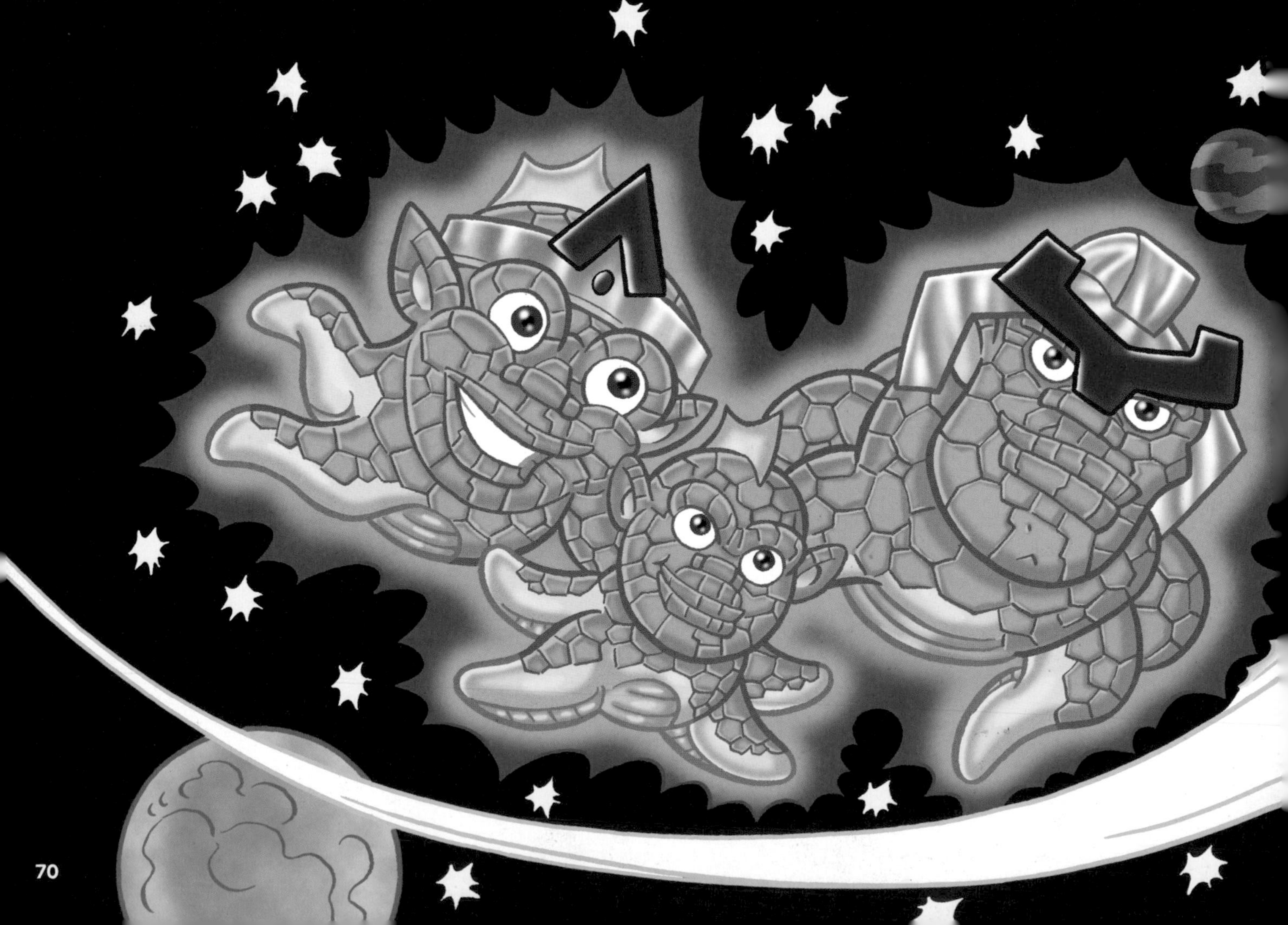

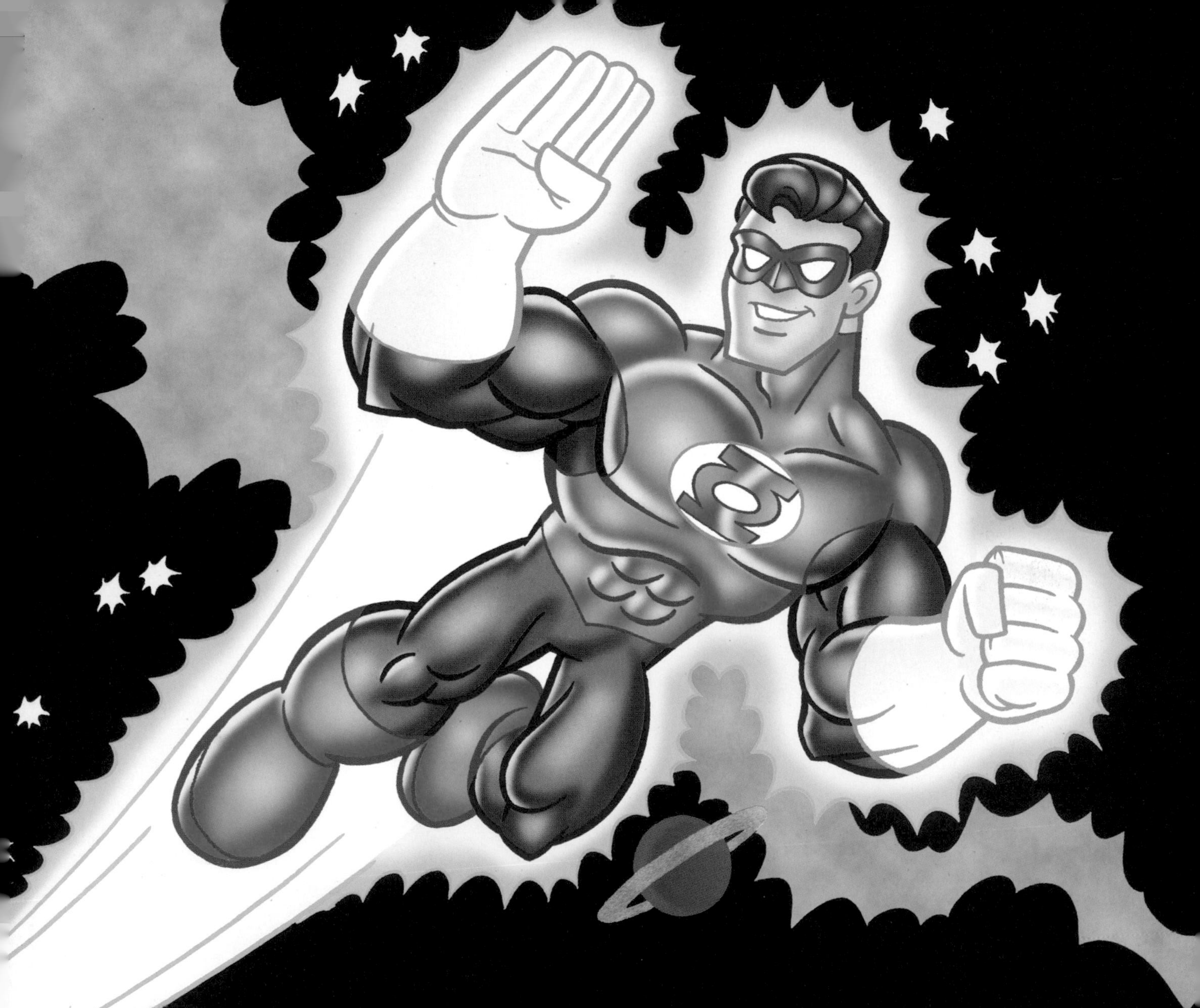

When they reached the edge of the solar system, Green Lantern waved to the aliens and shouted, "Have a safe journey, friends!"

Green Lantern returned to Earth, rocketing through the clear sky.
As he rejoined the other Super Friends, Batman said, "There's no time to lose. Joker and Mr. Freeze are taking over Gotham City."

"Let's go," Green Lantern replied. "Anything is better than babysitting!"

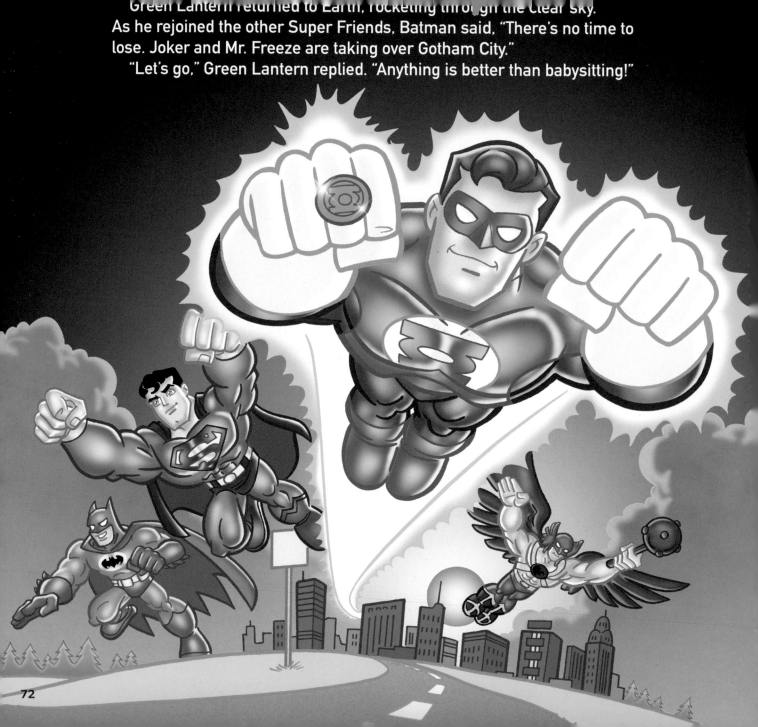

ATTACK OF THE ROBOT!

By Dennis "Rocket" Shealy

Illustrated by Erik Doescher, Mike DeCarlo,
and David Tanguay

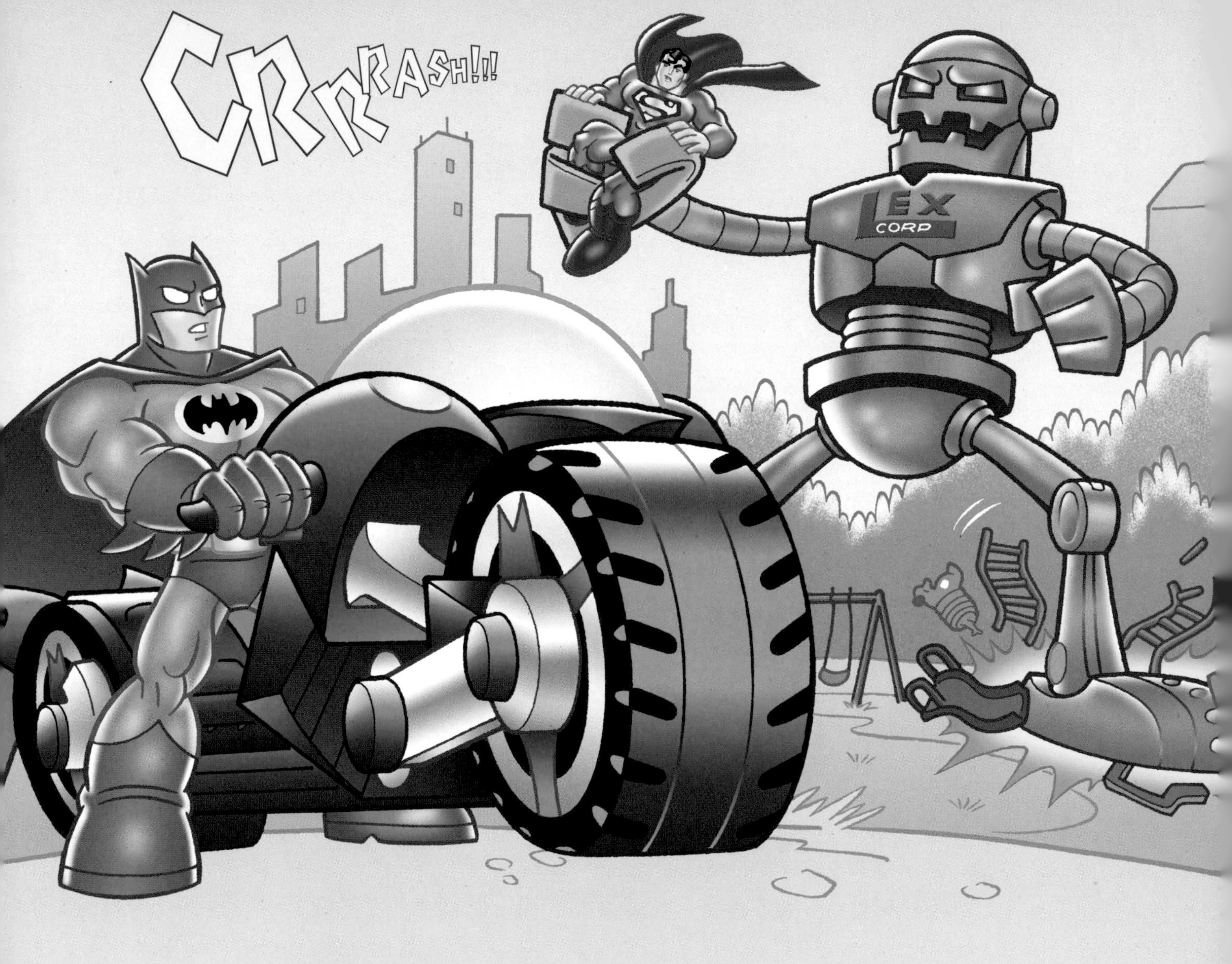
CRRRASH!!!
LEX CORP

Batman was patrolling the city on his Batcycle when he suddenly heard a terrible crash.

He looked up to see a giant robot. Superman was trapped in its mechanical Kryptonite claw!

"Kryptonite is the only thing that can harm Superman!" Batman said. "This looks like a job for the Super Friends."

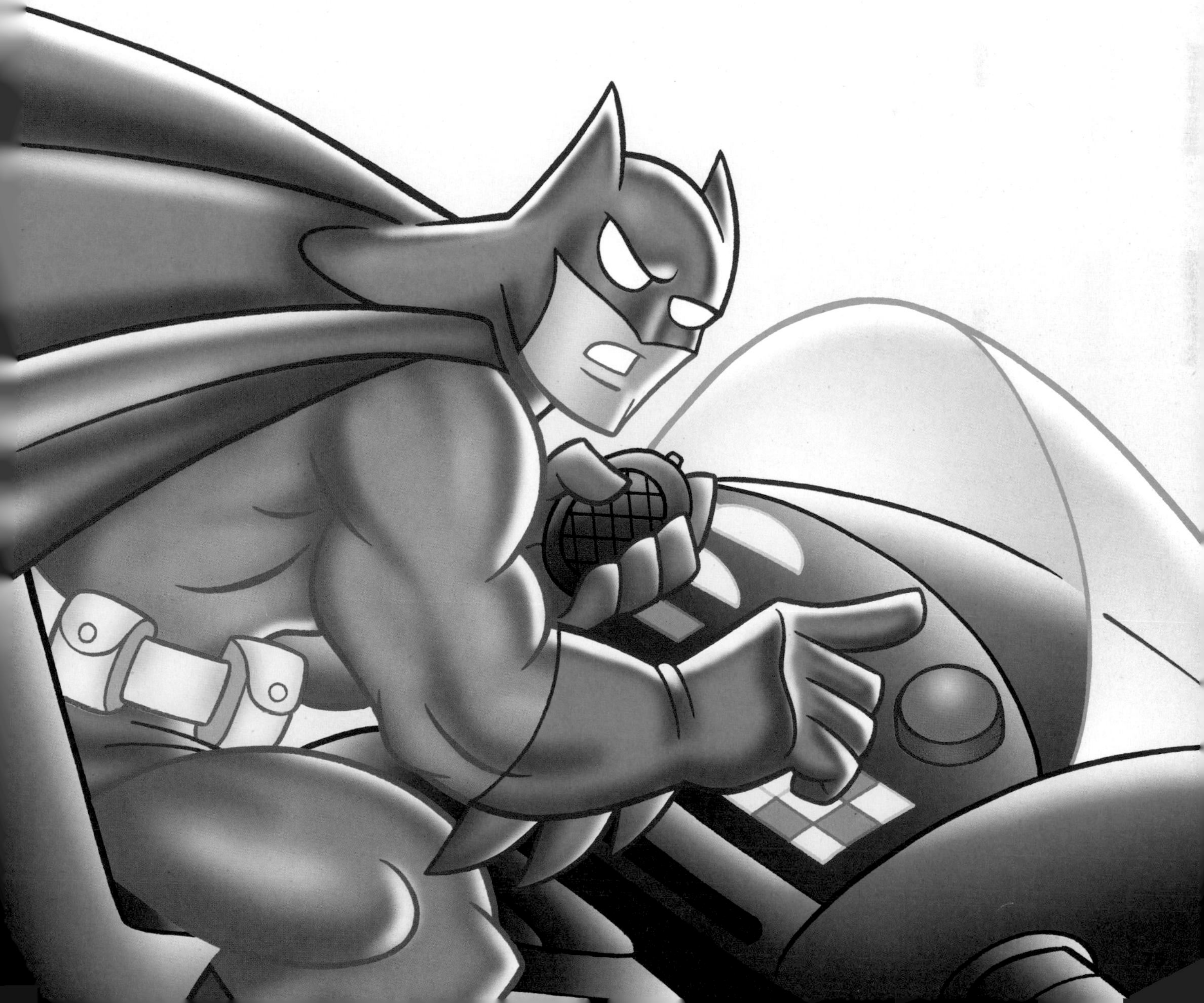

All across the world, the Flash, Aquaman, and Green Lantern were busy helping people.

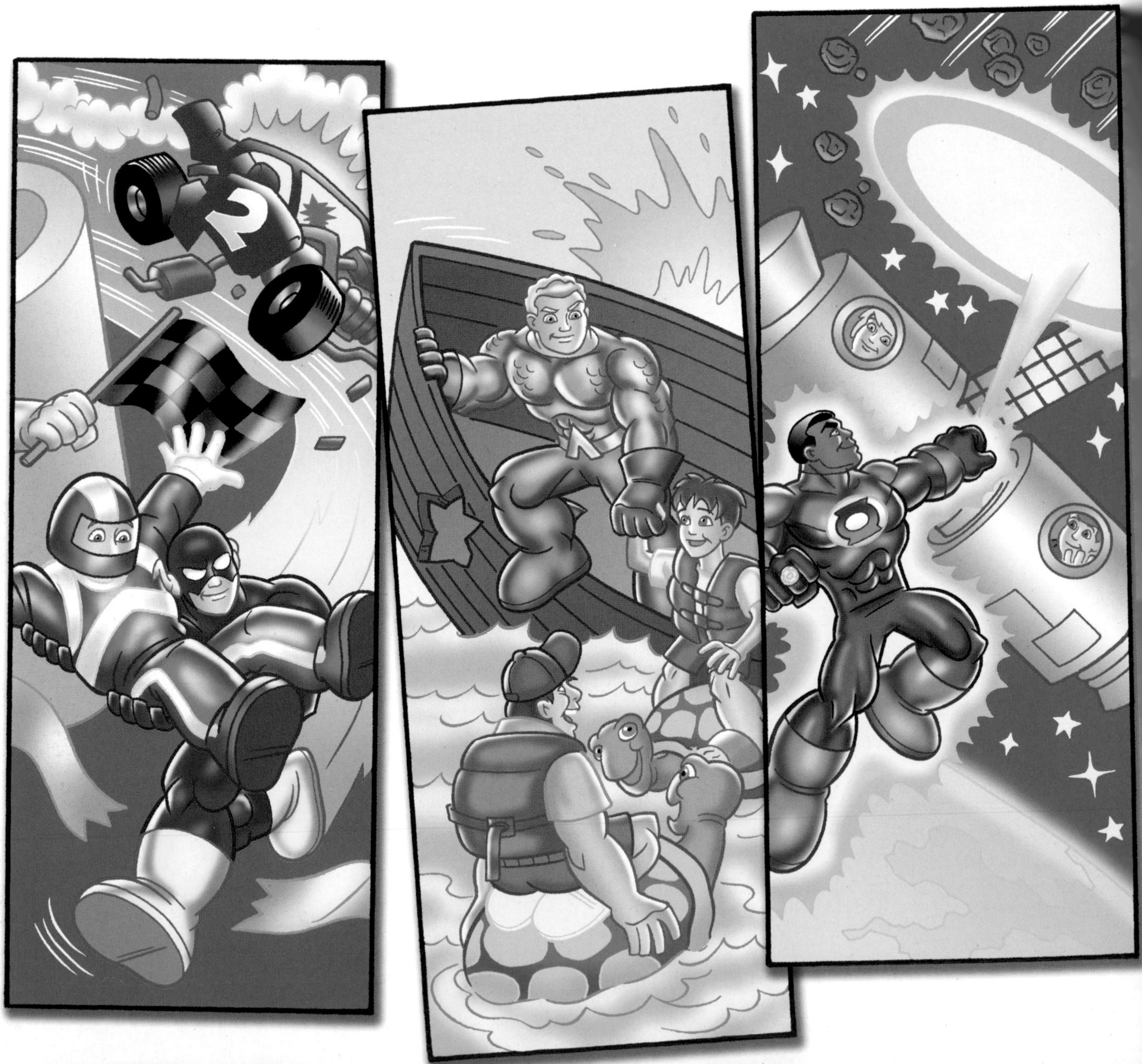
2

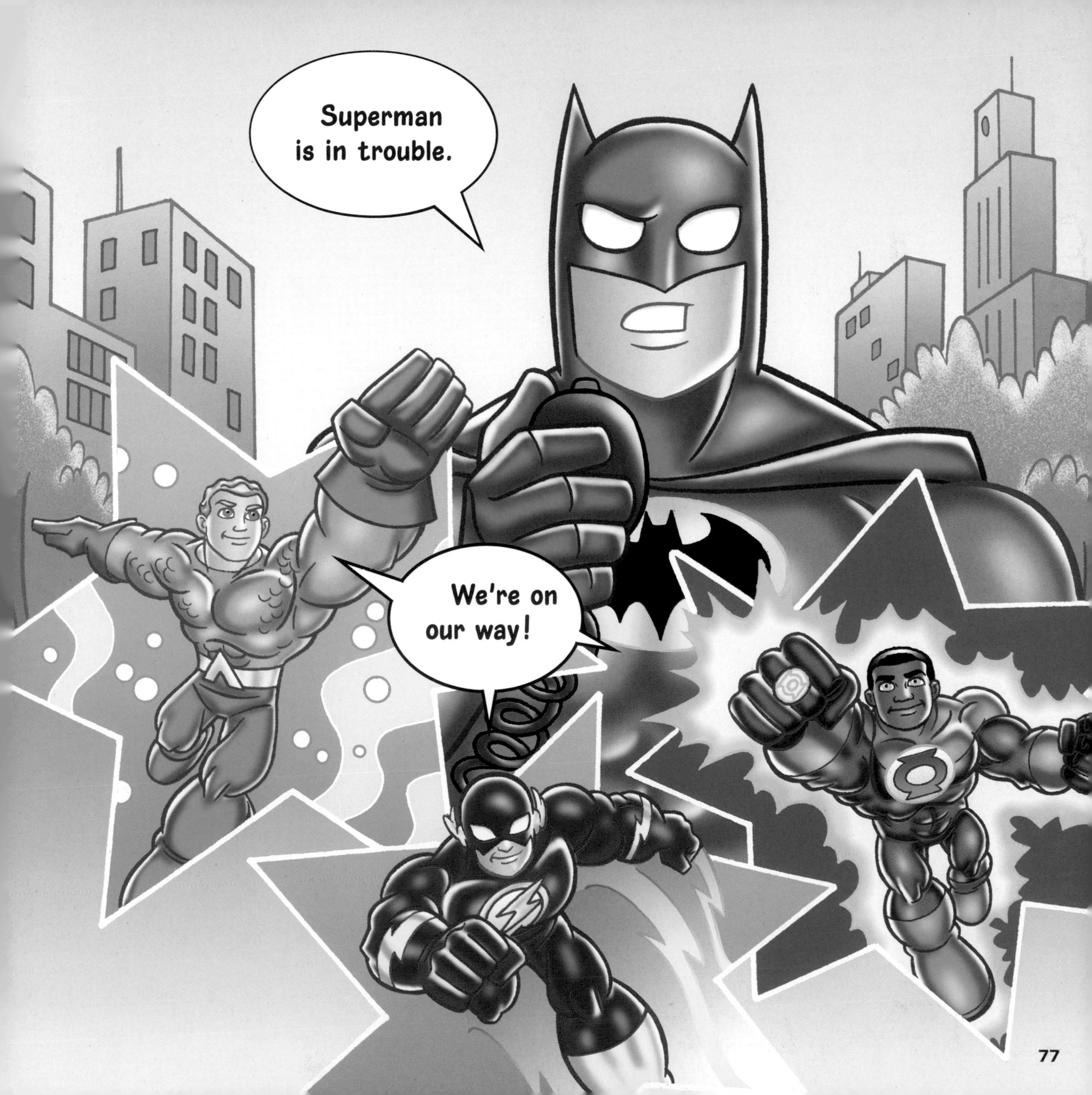
Superman is in trouble.
We're on our way!

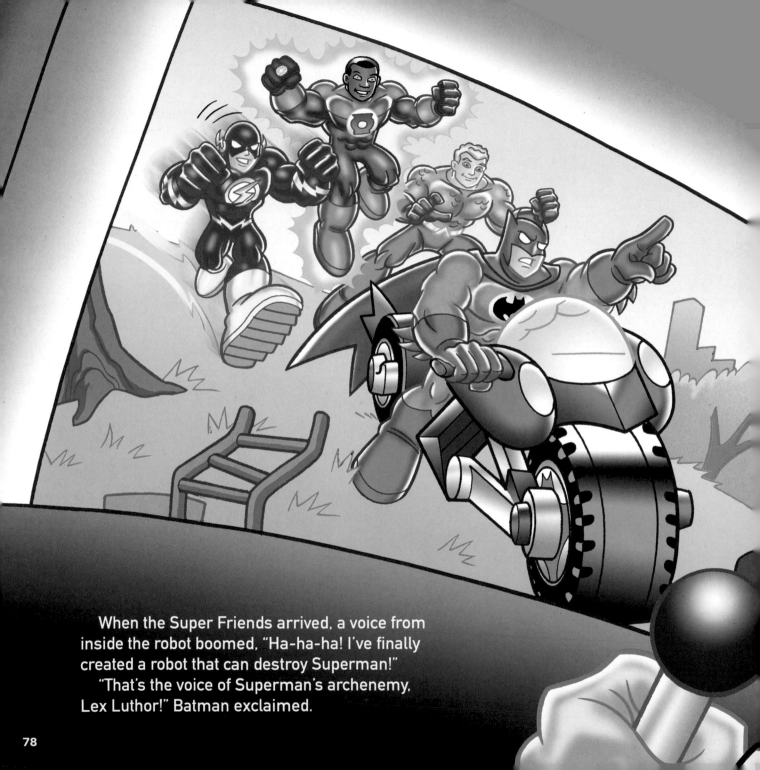

When the Super Friends arrived, a voice from inside the robot boomed, "Ha-ha-ha! I've finally created a robot that can destroy Superman!"

"That's the voice of Superman's archenemy, Lex Luthor!" Batman exclaimed.

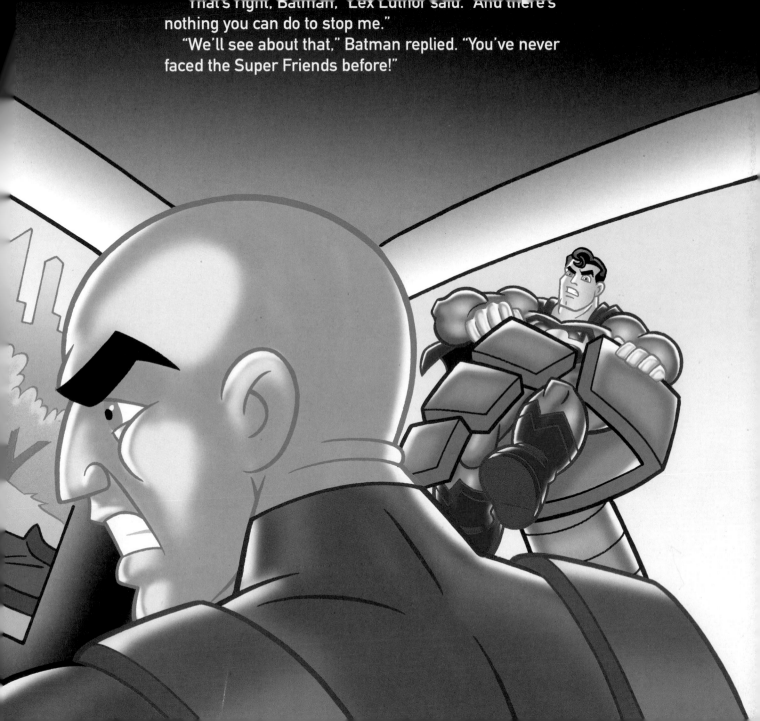

That's right, Batman," Lex Luthor said. "And there's nothing you can do to stop me."

"We'll see about that," Batman replied. "You've never faced the Super Friends before!"

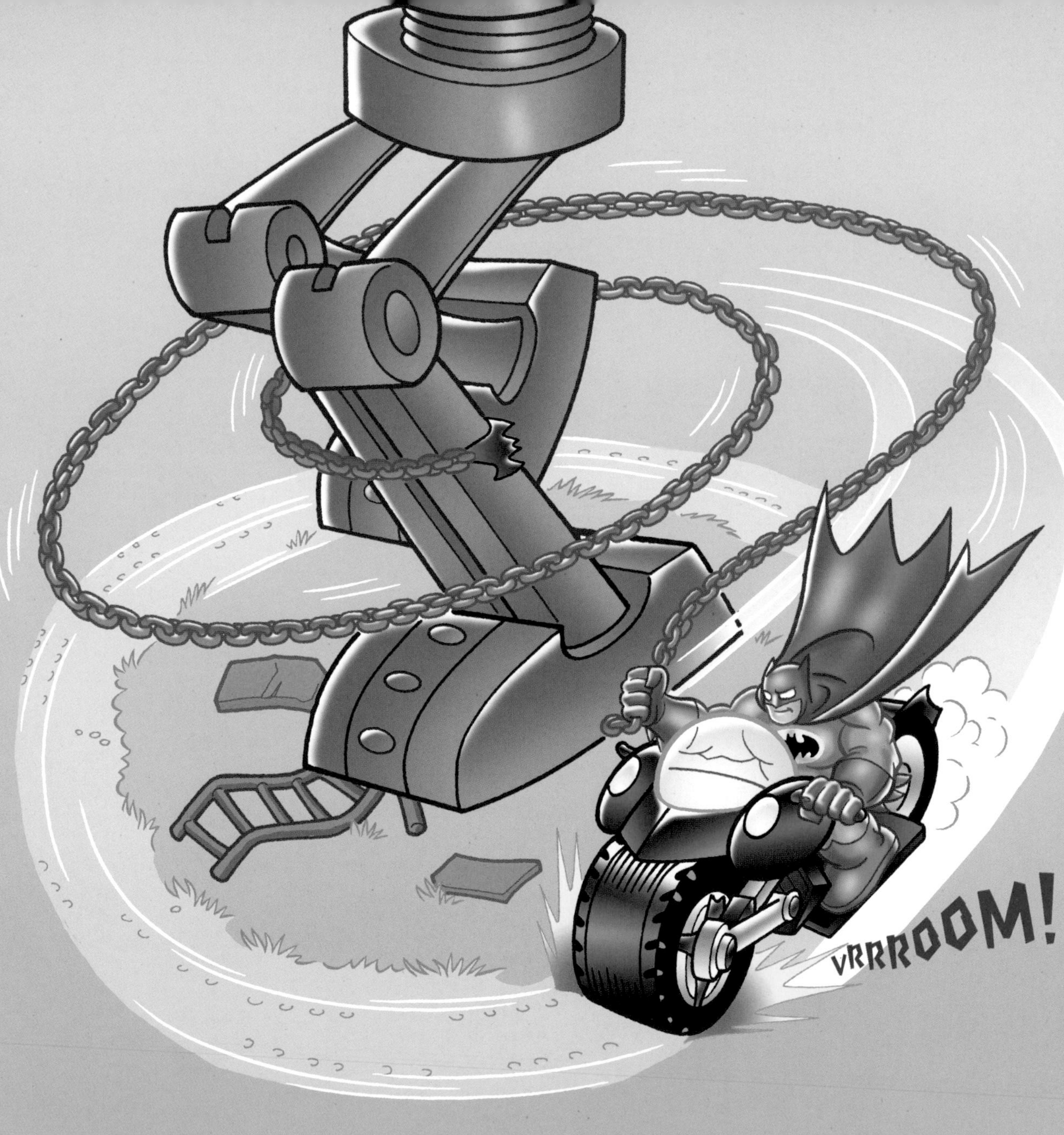
VRRROOM!

Batman signaled to the Super Friends. They each knew what to do. Batman attached a chain to the Batcycle and began to drive in circles around and around the robot's massive mechanical legs.

In a red blur of speed, the Flash raced up the robot and started removing all the bolts from the cruel Kryptonite claw holding Superman. There was nothing Lex Luthor could do—the Flash was just too fast!

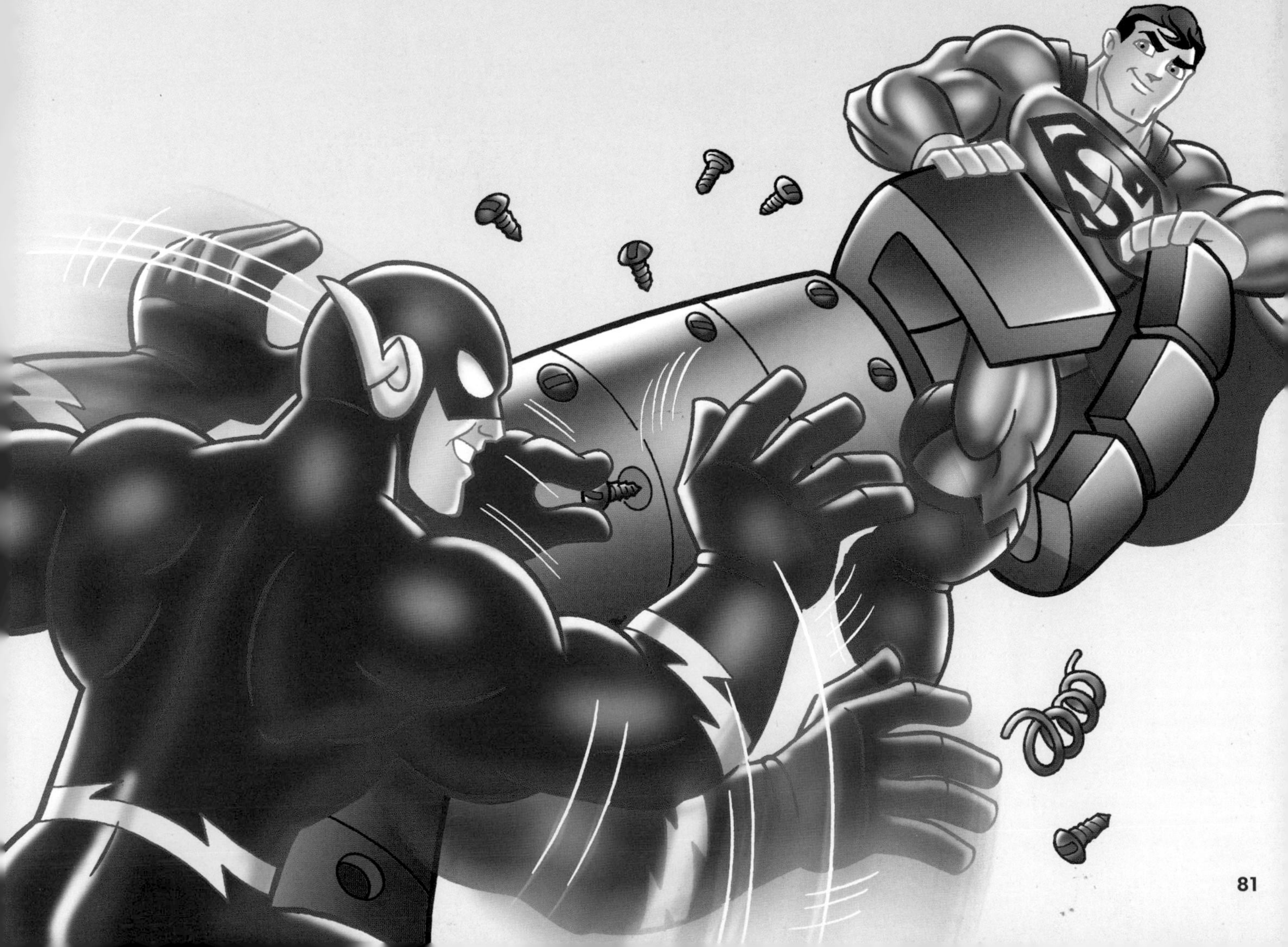

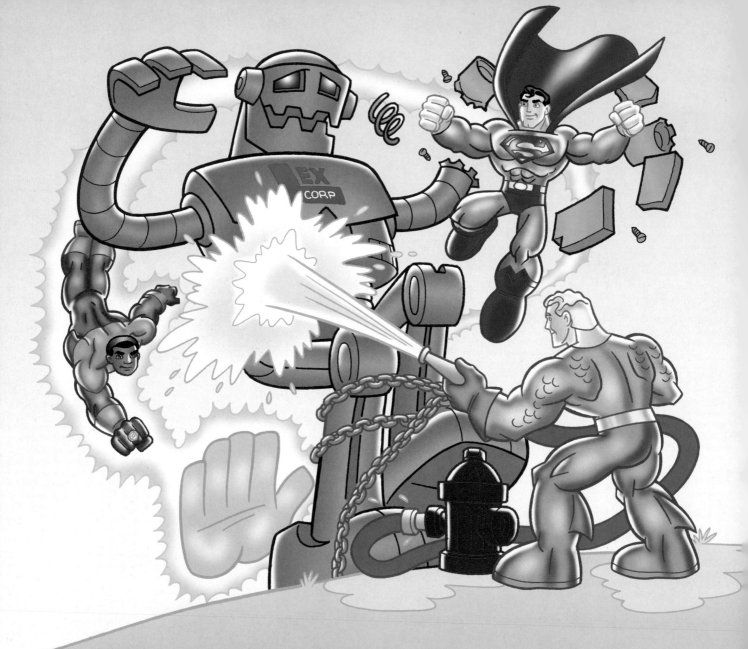

Aquaman opened a fire hydrant and directed a powerful blast of water at the robot's chest, knocking it off balance. Then Green Lantern created a glowing green hand with his power ring and pushed the robot over.

Superman broke free of the claw just as the robot came crashing down!

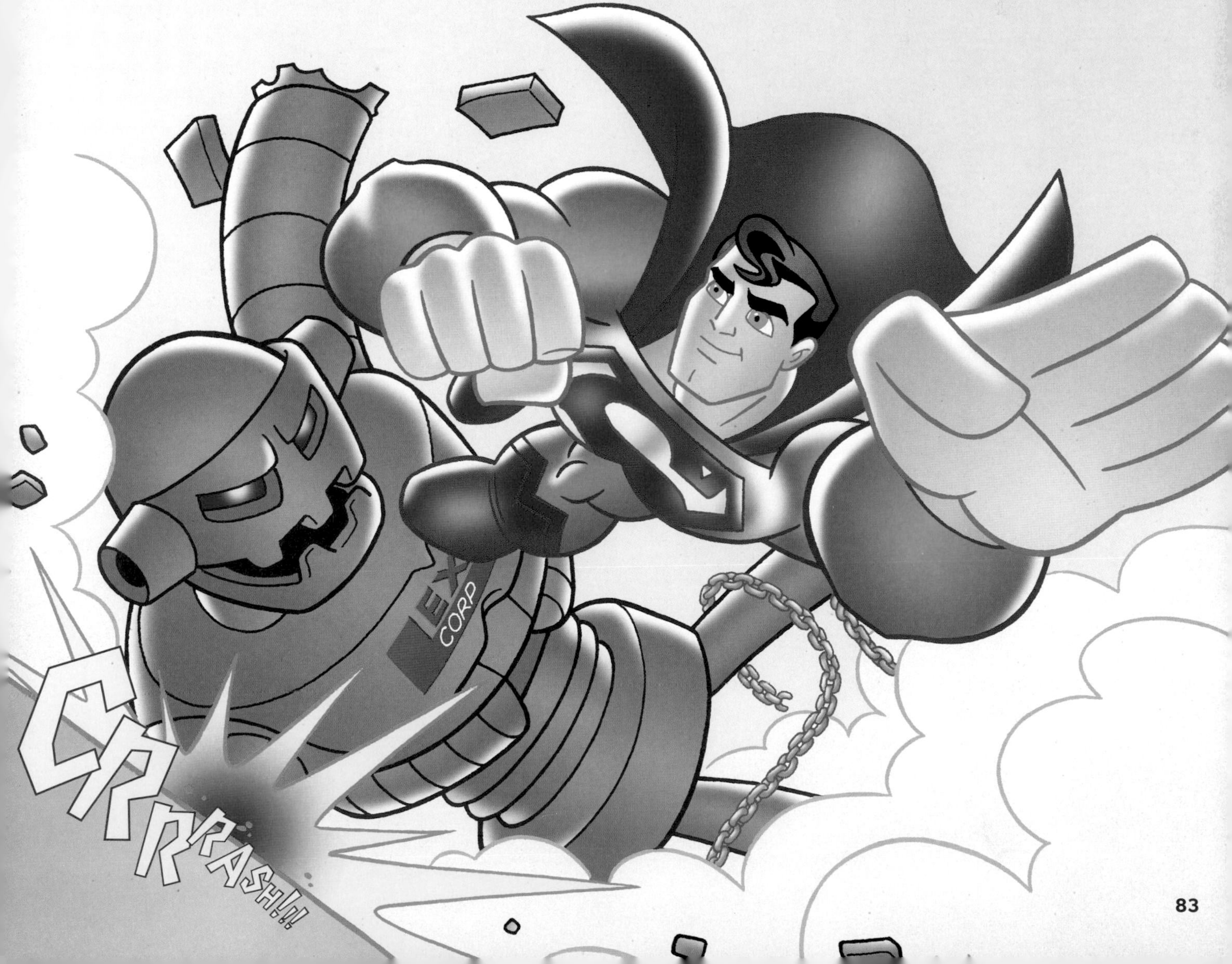

LEX CORP
CRRRASH!!!

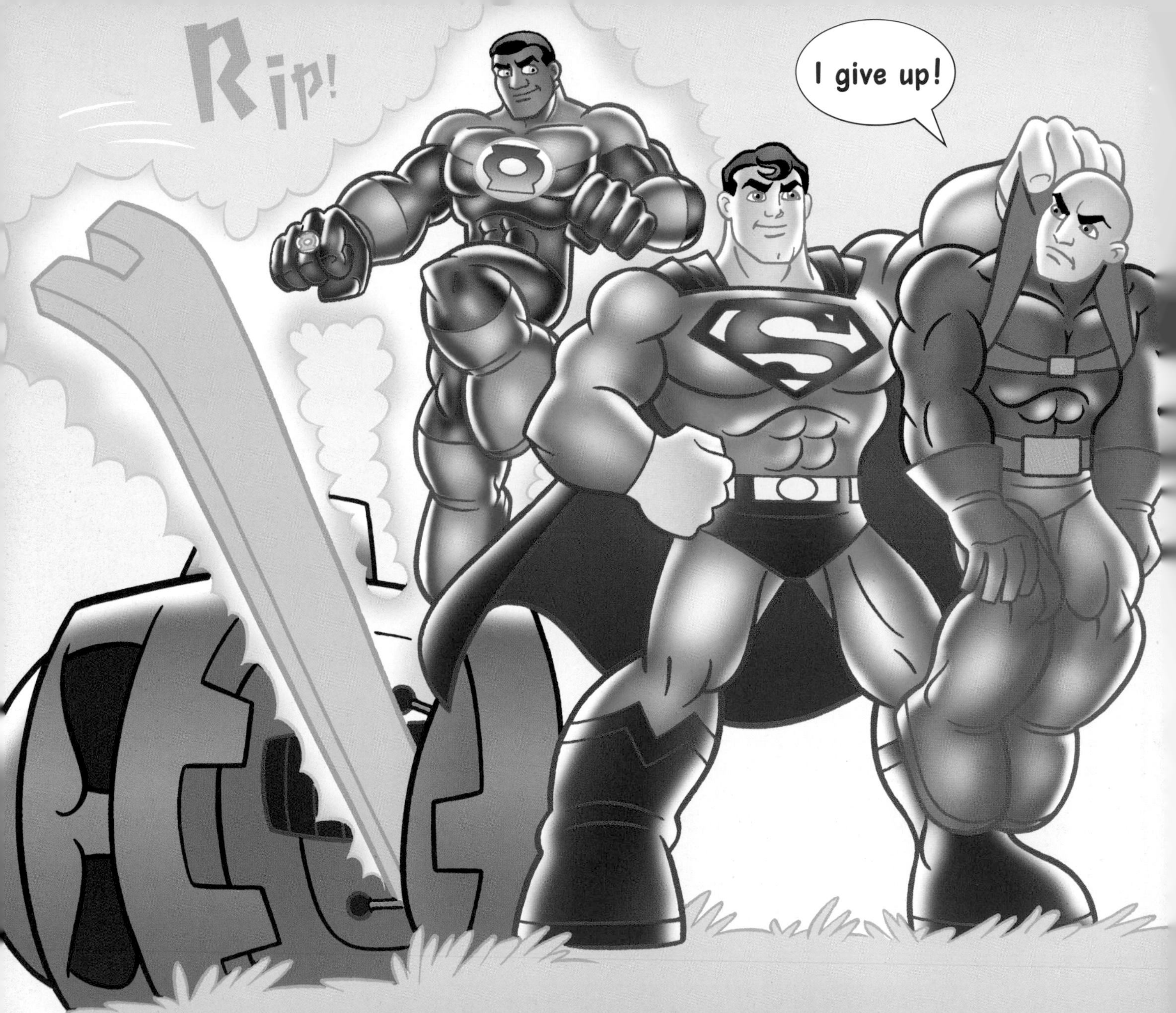
Rip!
I give up!

Green Lantern used his power ring to make a large crowbar and open the robot.

Superman easily lifted Lex Luthor out.

"But my robot was strong enough to defeat Superman," Lex Luthor groaned.

"When we work together as a team, we're unbeatable," Batman said, locking a pair of Batcuffs on the villain. "You can't defeat a super hero with friends—**Super Friends**!"

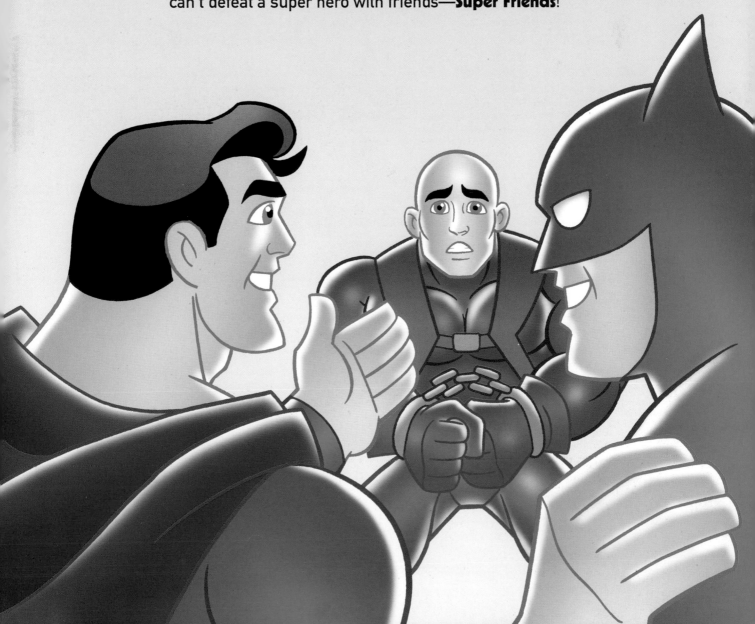

The Super Friends turned Lex Luthor over to the police, who took him to jail.

"Thanks for your help," Superman said to his teammates.

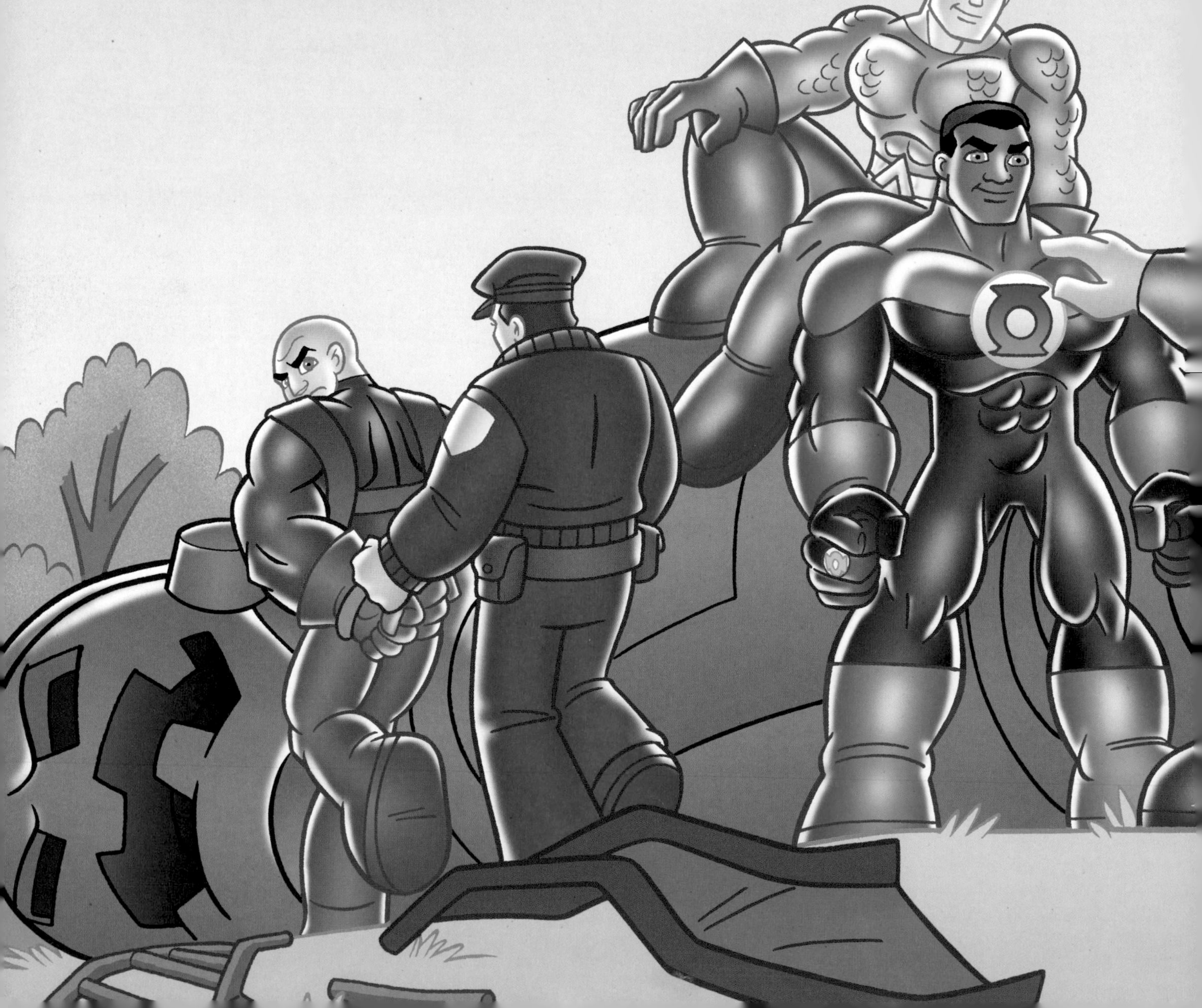

"Helping each other is what being Super Friends is all about," the Flash said. "But now what are we going to do with this robot?"

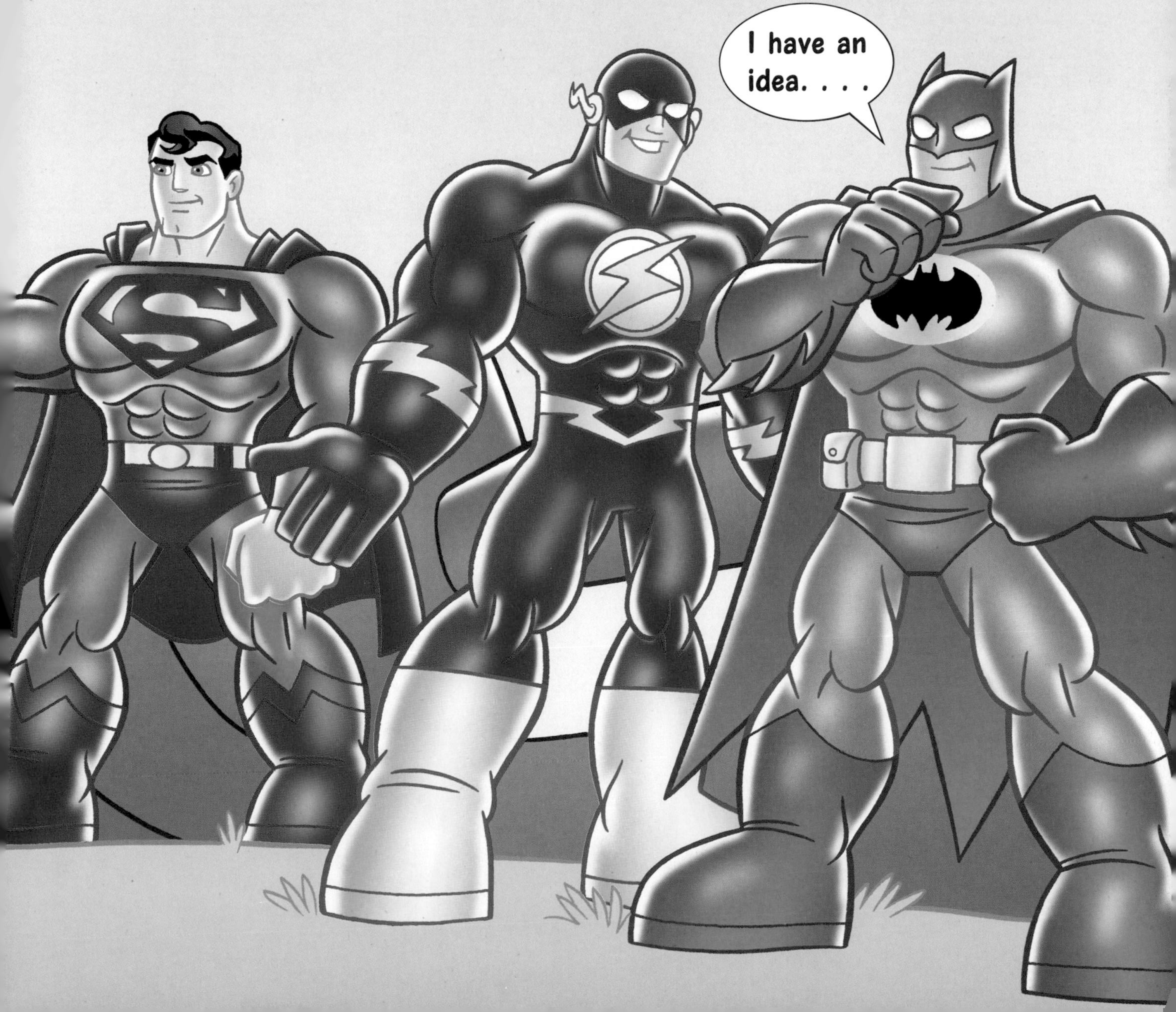
I have an idea. . . .

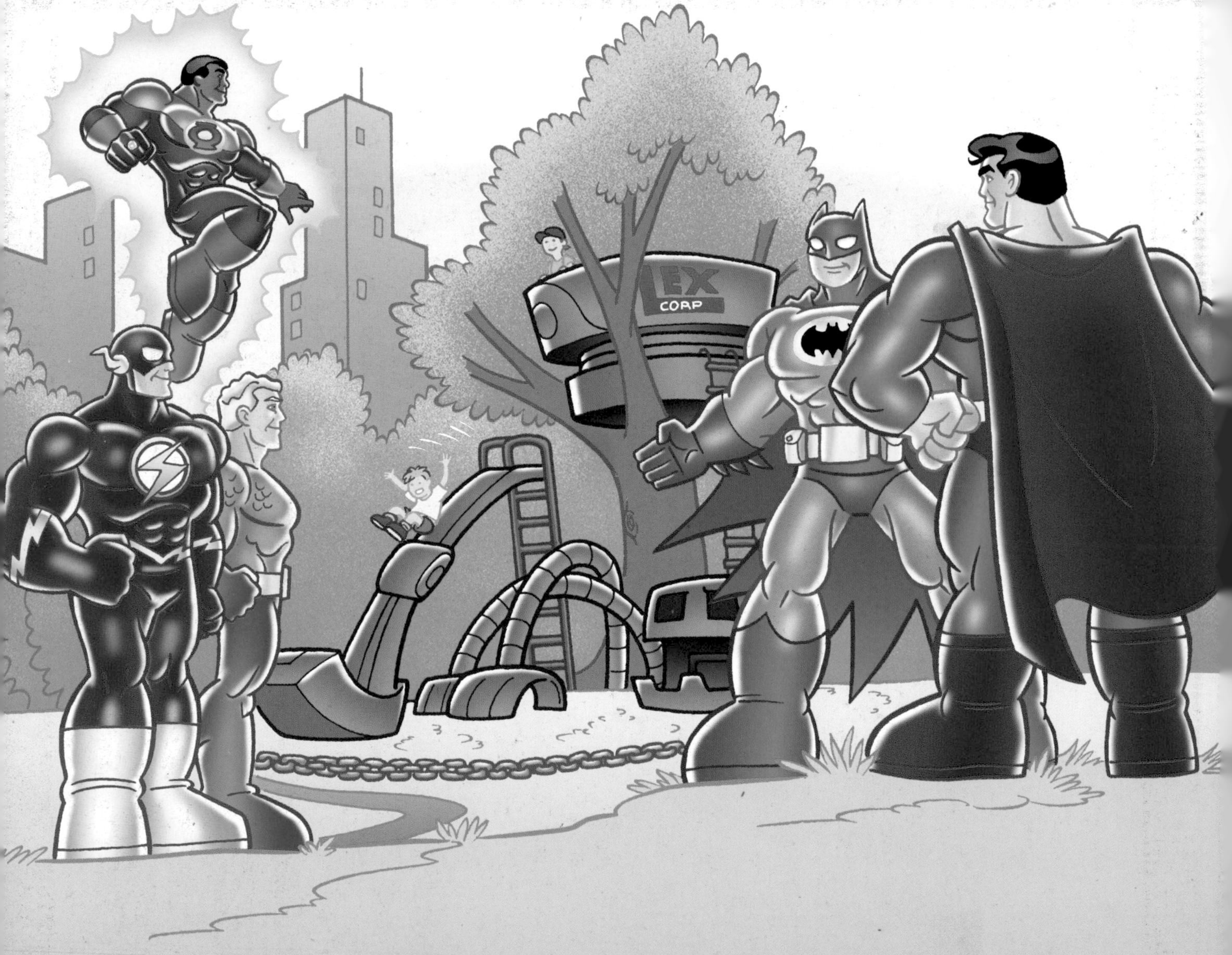
LEX
CORP

"Let's turn this mechanical menace into a timid tin man," Batman said.
And with that, the Super Friends used parts of the robot to rebuild the playground it had crushed. All the kids cheered. The Super Friends were the greatest heroes ever!